The Girl on the Bus

N.M. Brown

To Evan –
for believing that
this was possible !
love Dad

Print: 978-1-912175-15-4

'To my family, for your faith and patience'

Prologue

Claire Woods sighed as she carefully placed Rita back into her cushioned baby seat. Thankfully, after two hours in a hot car, she was almost asleep. It had been her seven-year-old son's helpful suggestion they take a break at the roadside services. The baking car had been like a glass prison for him, and when he spotted the red and white diner sign, it offered an escape to fresh air, and the promise of an iced soda.

As she struggled to manipulate the baby's arms through the webbing straps, Claire felt her son tug at her elbow. He stood restlessly next to her, wearing a yellow *Sponge Bob* t-shirt and blue denim shorts, as he moved helplessly from side to side.

'Hang on a minute, Daniel,' she said, trying to remain patient.

'I really need to use the bathroom,' he said, while squirming, and twisting his small fingers together.

'Don't be silly, you've just been.' Claire let out an aggravated breath, as she continued to fight against the unforgiving child harness.

Her statement was not entirely correct. After sitting in a red leather booth for the half hour it had taken Rita to reluctantly accept her bottle, Daniel had consumed two large cups of gassy Sprite. Claire had, therefore, assumed both her children would be full, and took the baby to the changing room, telling Daniel to come, too. Daniel, however, had recently reached that age where he was uncomfortable peeing in front of his mother. This was a humorous and poignant development for her, who had watched her liberated little boy dance around the house blissfully naked for most of his life. To accommodate his new-found modesty, Claire sent her son to use the gents' restroom, which was located beside the baby changing room. For added security, she left the door unlocked. Yet, rather than going to the bathroom, as agreed, Daniel – who was hopelessly attracted by all things glitzy – had stopped to gaze at the small cluster of arcade games. He had peered wide-eyed at the claw grab machine, which – as if sensing his presence- had spontaneously come to life. Daniel pressed his nose against the glass, and watched the silver claw judder to the centre of the cabinet, then descend, like the hand of a god, to pluck at the grinning stuffed toys below.

As Daniel stood hypnotized by the metallic claw, Claire eventually approached him with a look of triumph on her face. Rita was finally sleeping. Claire held a finger up to her lips and nodded her head towards the exit.

It wasn't until they were already at the car the boy realised he had forgotten to go the bathroom, and his full bladder felt swollen and painful.

At first, Daniel thought he could possibly hold on with his legs crossed until the next comfort break, but his body was already struggling to contain the fluid. This was what convinced him to tug his mother's elbow, as she arranged Rita in her seat.

Claire looked down at Rita, who was, for the moment, still asleep. To risk taking her back inside, and reawakening the beast, was not a viable option, but neither was leaving her in the busy car park. Over the years, Claire had heard enough horror stories about babies being snatched from public places, or about social services getting involved when an infant had been left in a car for mere minutes. Her only option was to get Daniel to hurry into the toilets, while Claire watched from the driver's seat. He was a sensible boy, and even aged four, he had received the Gingerbread Kindergarten prize for road sense.

'Okay.' Claire stood up, and peered across the three rows of parked cars and buses to the building, 'I can't leave Rita, and if I lift her she will probably wake up. You know that, don't you?'

'Yeah,' her son replied, and nodded vigorously.

'So,' she continued, 'I'm going to let you go yourself, okay?'

'Sure,' Daniel said quickly.

'Now, the toilets are just inside the entrance, over there,' Claire said slowly, as she pointed to the double doors.

Her restless son nodded enthusiastically.

'It's the first door inside.'

'I know.' Daniel squirmed some more. 'We've just been there.'

'Well, you go back in yourself, watch out for cars, and use the crossing point. Okay?'

'Okay,' Daniel whined, and hurried off.

Keeping her eyes locked on her son, Claire climbed into the warm seat of the Toyota Camry. She followed her son's journey, as he snaked through the labyrinth of cars. He moved quickly between a Lexus and a Ford Focus, then disappeared between two coaches, only to reappear a moment later at the crossing point. Claire watched the doorway of the building for a few minutes. Behind her, Rita began to snore lightly. In the fleeting moments that Daniel was lost from sight, dark fears appeared like storm clouds around the fringes of Clare's mind. However, they were quickly dispelled by the reappearance of her son, a moment later, in the doorway of the service station. Holding up one hand, he waved proudly to his mother, and then purposely checked the road before crossing. Claire exhaled, then smiled, and turned around to check on her sleeping baby.

It was in that fleeting instant, Daniel Woods vanished.

It had been the *Ben 10* alien figure which had caught his attention, like a glittering hook in some murky depths. Having crossed the road safely, the boy walked purposely through the space between two buses. Hidden from the afternoon sun, the corridor formed by the long, silver vehicles was cool, like a shadowy ravine. Although, it was not lifeless - the two coaches were gently shuddering, as if they were great sleeping beasts.

Halfway along the strange alleyway, Daniel noticed one bus had its long luggage compartment open. The flap covering the cavity had been lifted up, and pushed back to rest against the side of the bus. This had exposed a deep, dark cavity in the belly of the vehicle. Daniel thought it looked like an open doorway, lying on its side.

As he drew level with the long cavity, Daniel's curiosity overwhelmed him. Crouching down - as if to waddle duck-like - he peered into the chamber beneath the bus. What he saw there in the shadows made him gasp. The cavity was almost entirely empty, with the exception of a red plastic crate shoved against the back corner of the space. The crate overflowed with brightly coloured toys and candy. Action figures and Barbie dolls were stretching out of a tangle of Slinky Springs, jewellery sets and Hot Wheels cars. Around the outside of the plastic box a selection of *Ben 10* - Daniel's current favourite - figures were scattered around. The sight reminded him of pictures of Santa's sleigh. Only this wasn't December; it was July.

The temptation placed before the boy was simply too much. He knew his mom would be waiting, so he had to be quick. Daniel glanced furtively back over his shoulder, then happy enough with the lack of witnesses, he climbed into the cool rectangular compartment. Within the shadowy crawl space, there was a faint smell which reminded Daniel of the large white medical room at his kindergarten. Crawling over towards the box of toys, the small boy made a quick grab for a Rip-jaws figure, but as his fingers closed around the figure, someone slammed the door of the compartment shut- trapping him inside.

Claire was out of the locked car now, and running crazily back and forward calling her son's name. Her efforts were undermined by the dull blasting horn of some large vehicle, which was regularly obliterating her cries. Cold fear began to flood her body, as she darted around the sea of cars. Seeing no sign of her son, Claire dropped to her knees on the hot asphalt, and looked desperately beneath the sea of cars in the hope of glimpsing red, size five baseball boots wandering by. *Maybe he's just lost*, she repeated to herself, in a tenuous mantra. Standing up, she began to stop random strangers, clutching their arms in swelling desperation.

'Have you seen a little boy?' she asked repeatedly, her voice rising to a panicky crescendo.

Suddenly, Claire formed a notion of hope. Perhaps he had simply returned to the bathroom. Tracing Daniel's initial route, she ran back to the service building. Pushing the male bathroom door open, and with no regard now for propriety, Claire found nothing but empty cubicles.

'Are you okay?' asked a female employee, who appeared over her shoulder, wearing a red cotton vest, and carrying a plastic clipboard.

'I've lost my son,' Claire blurted through a ripple of hot tears. 'He's just seven years old.'

'Okay,' the woman spoke calmly. 'Let me help you. What's his name?'

'It's Daniel,' Claire gasped.

As the woman spoke into a small radio clipped to her lapel, Claire hurried back outside, and ran over to the Toyota. By now, she was making all sorts of deals with God to let her find her son standing nonchalantly at the side of the car. As she reached the vehicle, she discovered only Rita, blissfully oblivious of the chaos unravelling around her.

Around Claire, a group of hastily organised employees began to sweep systematically through the parking lot. Seeing this unfold, she felt a new wave of desperation wash over her. Cupping her hands to her mouth, she began shout her son's name relentlessly. Rushing randomly from car to car, her calls were still regularly punctuated by the angry blasts of some air horn. Whilst the minutes passed, Clare's shouting gave way to screaming her son's name, until her voice grew hoarse, and there was finally no breath left.

It was then, in the hopeless silence, a sound formed, like a flare in an eternity of darkness. The broken mother thought she heard her lost son call out to her.

Pausing, Clare's eyes widened, and then, she heard the sound again - faint, but enough. She moved closer to the sound, passing cautiously by a rusty Volvo, and then, a Lexus.

Claire was vaguely aware the blasting of the horn was louder now, and coming from a large silver bus, which was angrily lurching inches forward. A refrigerated truck, with European plates, had entered the parking lot on the wrong side of the road, and had stopped in front of the service area, blocking the exit of all other vehicles - including the impatient bus. But, it was then, in the small silences between the raging snorts of the horn, Claire heard her son's muffled voice. She felt her heart stutter, and, operating on some instinctive level, she followed the sound to the side of the bus. Kneeling on the hot ground, she was oblivious to the diesel staining the knees of her cream pants, as she put her ear to the side of the juddering vehicle.

For what seemed like a hopeless eternity, there was nothing, and Claire felt a knot of despair form deep inside her body. Tears dripped from her face on to the hot tar of the parking lot, and she felt herself slip out of reality.

Then, a loud banging from within the bus jolted her back to life.

'Mom?' a small, scared voice said.

'He's here!' she screamed. Her voice was loud and strong enough to wash out over the car park, like a wave of maternal instinct.

Despite this, for years following the incident, Claire would dream about this moment - only, in the syrupy paralysis of nightmares, no sound would come forth from her barren throat, and she would claw weakly at the metal flanks of the departing bus, while it stole her child away.

The woman with the clipboard hurried across the parking lot, and stood officiously in front of the bus, with her hands held up. The bus engine finally died, and the door hissed angrily open.

Claire was vaguely aware of the people who gathered around her, as she frantically grabbed at the handle of the luggage compartment, ripping off one of her nails in the process.

An elderly man wearing a bus company uniform leaned in front of her, and inserted a small stubby key into the body of the bus. He ushered people back, and opened the compartment. Daniel scampered out of the darkness, and into his mother's arms. His face was streaked with tears, and a damp patch had darkened his denim shorts. His mother buried her face in his neck, and sobbed and sobbed. She cast her puffy eyes towards the Californian sky, where a small god had a change of cruel heart.

The elderly bus driver, who appeared to be as rattled by the experience as Daniel, was busy telling everyone he had just loaded a bundle of toys into the hold for his twin son and daughter's birthday.

'I swear, I only went for a smoke,' he said in a dazed voice. 'I should have checked again.'

A small smattering of passengers, who had also descended from the bus, confirmed they had collectively known nothing of the small stowaway.

But, the crowd of onlookers were only interested in the happy reunion in front of them. As the audience separated and returned to normality, Claire and Daniel made their way back to the car, where the baby remained locked in oblivious sleep. Daniel, who was being carried, had his arm curled around his mother's neck. As they moved through the lanes of cars, the boy smiled and waved at the bus driver, who offered a relieved grin, and waved back at the departing child and his mother.

However, once they were out of sight, the elderly driver's expression changed to that of pained frustration. He turned to one of the passengers - a large man wearing a Hawaiian shirt - and patted his broad shoulder.

'It's okay, Wendell,' he said softly. 'We'll have plenty more chances.'

1

Vicki had already picked up the telephone handset and quickly replaced it three times, before she finally summoned the confidence to fully dial the number. She was sitting in front of the green-glass dining table, in what had once been, prior to the divorce, her parents' beach apartment. It was a tasteful, single storey building, with smooth whitewashed walls, and a small balcony overlooking the booming ocean. A wooden deck led directly on to the bone coloured beach. If Vicki actually allowed herself to, she could remember countless seasons spent here in the cool, white sanctuary. Looking out through the patio window, she could see the sun-bleached balcony, where she had often sat as a child, blanket-wrapped upon her father's knee, watching shooting stars streak above the sea, while her mother sat comfortably inside, sipping Earl Grey tea. Her father had pointed out constellations, and told her everybody's lives were written in the stars, like a secret message only some people knew how to read.

But, now, she chose not to think about that; her past had been a lie.

In front of her, on the table was an iPad displaying a moving slide-show of photographs featuring two smiling female students. Gazing intently at the pictures as they faded smoothly from one to another, Vicki barely recognized her own image, and found herself in the bizarre position of being envious of her own life - or at least, of the one presented on the screen. The photographs had been taken three and four years earlier, so she looked younger, obviously, but the difference was more than simply superficial.

Back then, Vicki had been optimistic about the world and life - and this had shown in her untroubled eyes. Partly she'd taken confidence by osmosis from the girl standing by her side in many of the photographs. They had been physically alike - petite with long light brown hair - and many of the other students had assumed they were sisters, but this shared physicality was their only similarity; at least, initially.

Vicki was a mouse-like, self-conscious young woman, whereas Laurie was confident and strong. She had to be. When she had been six years old, her father had gone out to buy some cigarettes and never returned. Laurie's mother responded to this sudden change in circumstance by sinking progressively into a cave of clinical depression. Therefore, throughout most of Laurie's childhood, she served as the emotional support for her mother, rather than the other way around. She told Vicki how she would often come home from school to find her mother in the dark bedroom, sitting in her nightgown, with an overflowing ashtray on one side, and her wedding photograph album on the other.

Therefore, Laurie' upbringing, or lack of it, meant that she was both self-reliant and forgiving of other people's flaws. Without the financial security of her family, she had managed to complete all of her assignments, whist maintaining an almost full-time job as a cocktail waitress in Jimmy Love's Restaurant.

One Halloween, during the Social Studies Spooktacular Ball, Vicki and Laurie had excitedly dressed in matching zombie costumes purchased from Walmart, which made it impossible for anyone to tell them apart. Over the course of the evening, they had relished switching identities – Laurie was able to fade comfortably into the background, and Vicki got to adopt an air of confidence entirely foreign to her. She had moved crazily on the dance floor and made out with at least two masked men.

Now, in the sterility of the silent beach house, Vicki's past seemed like another life - one she yearned to somehow recreate.

Vicki hesitantly dialled the number, brushed her fringe from her eyes, and held the phone to her ear.

'Hello?' the voice sounded unchanged since the last time Vicki had heard it.

'Hi, Laurie?'

'Yep?'

'It's Vicki.' She paused. 'Vicki Reiner.'

In the momentary silence that followed, she anticipated the horror of Laurie failing to remember her at all. Perhaps the friendship had been nothing more than the convenience of sharing a living space, and Vicki had magnified it in her mind. However, her doubts were dispelled, when she heard Laurie squeal with delight.

'Oh my god, Vicki, how are you, girl?'

On the other end of the line, Vicki felt a mental sigh of relief.

'I'm good,' she lied. 'How are you doing? What you up to?'

'Ah, you know me. Same old underachiever, but with a little bit of style. I'm flipping burgers for six bucks an hour. Where are you?'

'Still in Oceanside, still being a parasite, and still bumming around at my parents' empty house.'

'Well, babe, don't you go beating yourself up about it. If I was down there on the Californian shore, I'd never want to leave, either.'

'Actually, that's why I'm calling,' Vicki said, and took a deep breath.

'Yeah?'

'You fancy coming down to stay for a break, just for a change of scenery?'

'You mean it?' Laurie said in a breathless voice.

'I really, really mean it.'

'Hell yes!' Laurie screamed with delight.

2

At the same time as the sausages were starting to brown beneath the gas grill, Dennis McLean poured a ladle of golden corn oil onto the large griddle, and spread it around with an old three-inch paint brush he kept in a plastic jug next the hob for just this reason. He was a big man, and at sixty-seven years old, he was starting to carry his spreading weight like an uncomfortable burden. His wife was forever telling him to lay off the red meat, but with his own walk-in cold store filled with every type of animal, cutting back on the flesh was not an easy option.

As the oil began hiss and splatter, Dennis went to the double refrigerator and removed a rectangular Tupperware box. He then laid out several slices of streaky bacon on the hot griddle, and glanced through the emerging smoke at the numerous bodies filling the booth seats. Eddie Gee's Diner had, as far as the chef could recall, never been so busy at 10:00 a.m. on a Monday morning. It was a small place, located three miles off the interstate, and run solely by Dennis. He would take care of the place up until noon, when his temperamental sister-in-law would help out. Although her version of helping basically involved standing at the back of the fire escape, smoking menthol cigarettes, and occasionally carrying plates of food to ravenous customers - if she felt like it.

Most early mornings the diner had a steamy rush of customers – mainly fruit pickers and farmhands - from around 7:05 a.m. until 8:40 a.m., after which things usually died down until around noon. But for some reason, today was different.

Just as Dennis had been using a grey cloth, peppered with coffee grounds, to wipe down the counter after the last of the breakfast customers had departed, the gruff rumble of the coach engine had caught his attention. He glanced up through the sheet glass windows to see the trembling silver vehicle sitting out on the parking lot, dominating the space like a big metal cuckoo. At first, he thought it was a Greyhound, lost off the highway, but on closer inspection he realised it was an older model than that.

The group of people who had emerged from the silver bus appeared to Dennis to be part of some tour, or maybe a business. The latter seemed less likely, given their mismatched appearance and lack of interaction with each other. Forming a steady stream of bodies, the visitors had come through the door, and spread around the place.

The travellers were all males, and had mostly asked for coffee – which was great, because this meant they could simply help themselves from the three Sunbeam coffee pots located on a hotplate to the side of the serving counter. However, two or three of the visitors had also requested hot food – bacon, sausage, and grits, mostly.

Dennis used a single, practised hand to break each of the six eggs from a pack into a plastic jug, then stirred in half a quart of cream. He added a couple of handfuls of Longhorn cheese, and then poured this into a cast iron frying pan. As the mixture bubbled, he walked to the counter, and glanced at the cheques pegged on the wire. If it had been a normal morning, he wouldn't have used paper orders – relying instead on his rusty old brain - but today, it was a necessary evil, with two dozen strangers descending on the place like a plague.

Dennis turned off the grill and plated up the food, placing each dish under the hot lights. He came around front and carefully carried the meals to the customers. Once he was finished, he returned to the service bar, took down each of the paper orders, and - with a sense of accomplishment - impaled them on the brass bill spike at the far side of the counter.

Waddling back into the tiled kitchen area, Dennis poured himself a half cup of thick, black coffee, and grimaced as he swallowed the bitter liquid. He could remember a time when he could drink a litre pot dry in one morning, but three decades of fried food washed down with coffee and Jim Beam bourbon had eroded his guts.

He picked up a cloth and erratically wiped grease stains from the various surfaces, as he glanced curiously across at the group seated by the window. He was most fascinated by the role of the younger man, who sat with the coach party.

He had arrived on a green motorcycle about ten minutes after the bus. When he walked into the diner, all of the other customers nodded to him in acknowledgement, but he didn't appear to recognise any of them. He walked confidently to the counter, and asked Dennis for a coffee, then, while he was waiting for it, an elderly man came over to him and led him to a red leather booth seat where another two men were already seated.

The elderly man had instructed the newcomer to join them in taking a seat. For a moment, he glanced cautiously around, before he finally sat down on the opposite side of the table from the three men, whereas all of the other men from the bus were scattered around the diner.

The elderly man, a larger one in a Hawaiian shirt, and a scrawny figure in a Mickey Mouse hat sat opposite the young guy. It almost looked like the young buck was being interviewed for a job. As opposed to the rest of the customers, who looked on quietly, the *three amigos* - as Dennis now thought of them - seemed much more animated.

At one point, the young guy brought some type of flat computer from inside his jacket and laid in on the table. He worked his fingers across the screen, as the three amigos looked on with wide eyes. There was a great deal of explanation going on, with the young guy frowning and nodding.

During the conversation, the elderly man said something, and the youngster laughed loud enough to draw the attention of everyone in the building. The kid shook his head and stood up for a moment. Dennis figured the young guy was just about to leave, but the elderly man leaned towards him and quietly said something. Then, it was the turn of the large man in the

Hawaiian shirt to laugh, and the young guy's expression changed as he quickly sat back down again.

They got talking again, only this time Dennis figured the young guy looked much less comfortable than before. He said little, but nodded enthusiastically in response to everything the other three said to him.

At one point, mid-conversation, the Mickey Mouse guy glanced up, and spotted Dennis looking in their direction. He turned back to the group, and scribbled something down on a paper napkin, folding it in two and handing it to the large man. After skimming the napkin, he turned his head to look at the Dennis, and tapped his head in small salute. Dennis acknowledged the gesture with a small, self-conscious nod and focussed his attention on gathering up grease smeared plates and empty coffee cups.

Although Dennis stopped watching the group in the booth, the last thing he noticed was the elderly man slide a manila envelope across the table to the younger man. After that, the youngster left without touching his coffee. He crossed the parking area, climbed back on his bike, and departed in a cloud of dust and fumes. In his absence, the three amigos invited a few others from around the diner to join them at the table. When several new members had taken their seats in the booth, they all spoke quietly and intently. As Dennis busied himself with a mop – disinfecting the tiled floor behind the serving counter - he could only hear the general murmur of voices.

Eventually, the conversation in the window booth seemed to draw to a close. Without any specific announcement, the smattering of customers stood up and drifted out of the door towards the silent bus.

'Hey,' Dennis called to the departing travellers. 'What about the bill?'

'It's okay,' said a deep voice from over his shoulder.

Dennis turned around to find the large man in the Hawaiian shirt, standing a bit too closely behind him.

'I'll settle up for all of us,' he said, with a broad smile, and pulled out a brown leather wallet from his back pocket.

'Ah, that's good.' Dennis smiled, his face creasing into a labyrinth of wrinkles. 'For a moment, I thought I was about to get hustled.'

'Not at all,' the large man said. 'I just wanted to query one thing?'

'Yeah?'

'Who ordered that?' the large man asked, and pointed to the last bill on the spike.

As Dennis leaned over the metal sliver, narrowing his eyes, the large man moved with the speed and agility of experience. He grabbed Dennis's head in both hands and slammed it face-first on to the vertical spike. The large man twisted the head slightly, and held it there for a moment, as the chef's legs twitched and shook. Then, when the legs gave way completely, the large man allowed the body to slump to the floor. . He then leaned across the hot plate and picked up a piece of fried meat.

Tearing at the flesh with his teeth, the large man stood over Dennis McLean's body, until the spasms had dwindled to nothing. He bent down, taking the body by the feet, and then dragged it through the kitchen to the walk-in refrigerator.

Before the large man in the Hawaiian shirt left the diner, he dropped the lock on the door and tilted the hanging sign to "CLOSED."

3

At the dusty bus stop, on the edge of the cluster of lifeless homes known as Burke's End, Laurie-Ann Taylor sighed with relief, and blew her damp fringe away from her face. Her feet were hot and she badly needed to pee. But, now, relief was within sight - she could finally see the approaching bus in the distance.

The Greyhounds and Intercity coaches that occasionally growled along Route 15 through the parched landscape were generally fitted with air-con and toilets. There remained, however, a degree of uncertainty, because today she would be travelling with a lesser known bus company.

It had been almost one week since Vicki had called out of the blue, and invited her down to the coast for a break from small dusty boredom. In the fourteen months since graduating college in San Diego, Laurie had done nothing other than serve coffee and burritos in the sun-bleached diner of her home-town. Her patrons were mainly locals or the occasional marine from the military camp over at Barstow.

When she had first accepted the job, she had optimistically imagined she could bring her Nikon SLR to work, and between orders, she could take dramatic portraits of American diner life. In reality, any time between taking orders was spent cooking, mopping, and washing. The camera only came to work for one shift, and was subsequently returned to a crushed shoebox at the back of her cramped wardrobe.

With each passing month, Laurie's bright and ambitious college life seemed more like a vague dream than an actual memory - so the phone-call from her friend felt like a life line, thrown from the past. Vicki's parents were both professionals, who owned a holiday apartment on Oceanside, which she apparently practically lived in now.

After an hour of reminiscing about campus life, Vicki had promised Laurie she would drive up to meet her off the bus in Escondido, and they could continue catching up on the journey back to the beach.

Following the call, Laurie had sat cross-legged on her bed, with her laptop in front of her, and a large glass of cheap wine on the bedside table. She had performed a search on coach prices for her intended trip.

The route from Barstow, the nearest town to Burke's End, to Escondido was almost one hundred and fifty miles, and a journey of several hours. Most of the large companies charged similar prices for similar services. Laurie tried some smaller sites, too, but eventually, she settled upon taking a Greyhound, which at forty dollars for four and half hours of transport, seemed more than reasonable.

However, as Laurie typed in the details of her location and ticket type, a new pop-up box appeared on the screen in front of her. It was a bright yellow window, featuring a cartoon image of a bus grinning with dust clouds coming off its wheels. The text beneath the image said, "click here for a cheaper ticket." Laurie hit the "x" to close the window, but this only caused a full screen window to open featuring a business called Route King.

This page featured a list of bullet pointed benefits - unbeatable prices, fully air-conditioned buses, refundable tickets, and local pick up point. It was this final detail which appealed to her the most. It meant there was no need to get herself two miles east to the centre of Barstow. At the bottom of the page, in flashing red text, it stated the price of a ticket from Burke's End to Escondido was only twenty-five dollars. The offer was just too good to refuse. Laurie took a gulp of sweet pink wine, and clicked on the button marked "purchase tickets."

Now, three days later, the bus was approaching., Laurie checked her purse to secure her keys and cell phone whilst taking a step towards the baking road. The heat haze from the black-top was distorting the shape of the moving vehicle, melting it into little more than a grey and black mass. There was no wind to carry the distant rumbling sound, so as she narrowed her eyes against the afternoon sun the Route King bus appeared, like an approaching shark, moving silently through rippling air towards her.

As the bus reached within a hundred metres or so, Laurie slung her travel bag over one shoulder, and shielded her eyes. At first, she thought the bus wasn't going to stop. In her mind, she saw it sliding smoothly by, leaving her stranded in a cloud of cartoon dust – just like their logo. However, it began to slow and as the vehicle rumbled jolted to a stop, the doors hissed open. She stepped into the darkness and smiled – the interior of the vehicle was thankfully cooler than outside.

'Hey there.' The driver grinned at her from behind mirrored aviator sunglasses. He wore a denim shirt and Mickey Mouse baseball cap. 'Where you heading, sweetheart?'

'San Diego - Escondido,' she said, as she pulled a crumpled piece of paper bearing the *Route King* logo from her pocket and held it towards the man. 'I booked online.'

Taking the paper from her, the driver lowered his glasses and peered at it intently. His eyes scoured the details. Beneath his foot, the engine continued to growl impatiently.

'The website said to print off the details, and hand it to the driver,' Laurie said nervously.

A frown creased the man's face for a moment, then, the grin returned, and he slid his glasses back up his nose.

'Well, that all looks fine, miss. You go get yourself a seat and relax. Should be a fun trip.'

With that said, the driver turned back to the tinted windshield, pushed the gear stick and the bus lurched forward, leaving Laurie to stagger up the aisle. Having lurched from side-to-side, she slumped into the only available seat, and removed her bag. As she slipped her worn sandals from her hot feet, she had a brief glance around at her fellow passengers to check no-one appeared particularly offended by her actions.

The other travellers seemed to be oblivious to her – most were sleeping, listening to music, or staring out of the windows at the parched landscape. Directly opposite her, an elderly man with a neat moustache was reading a battered paperback edition of some Robert Bloch novel. He glanced at Laurie, smiled momentarily, then slipped back into the book.

Laurie glanced back up the aisle of the bus to see there was a bathroom halfway up. She decided she would give it a couple of minutes before she went. As she considered this, a man in the seat directly behind her leaned forward, and placed his hand on Laurie's headrest.

'Hi there,' he said, his voice deep and quiet.

Laurie said nothing.

'I said hi,' he continued, undaunted by her resistance.

'Hi.' Laurie turned around quickly, then back again. It was a quick gesture designed to show disinterest. There wasn't enough time to see his face, but she got the impression of a ruddy-faced man, with lank sandy hair and a wispy moustache. She reached for her bag and removed her iPod, unravelling the headphone cable. In her experience, earphones were a great way to shut out creeps.

'Where you heading?' he persisted.

'Nowhere,' Laurie said flatly, hoping he would take the hint and piss off.

'Looks to me like you're travelling all alone.' He whistled through his teeth. 'You're a brave young lady.'

'I won't be alone; I'm meeting my boyfriend.'

'But, not your only boyfriend, though…'

'What?' Laurie manoeuvred her body half around, with a frown on her face.

'Well, I don't see a ring on your finger,' the man said pointedly.

'What the hell are you trying to say?'

'No ring, so you're not married or engaged, either – makes you open to offers.'

'Look, mister, I'm not interested, okay? I just want to take a ride in peace.'

'Okay, okay, Little Miss Grumpy. I was only trying to break the ice a little.'

Laurie stared out of the window, trying to pretend she was interested in the dry desolation. It was like staring into an abyss.

The man behind her finally leaned back in his seat, leaving Laurie to listen to the groaning of the engine and the murmur of chatter. Now, she decided, would be a good time to the use the bathroom.

Making her way along the aisle towards the small bathroom stall, Laurie made only polite glances at the other passengers. There was nothing outwardly peculiar, but, as she glanced at the faces of the twenty-six commuters, she felt momentarily disturbed. It was not a conscious awareness, rather an instinctive feeling that something was missing. Perhaps it was simply there was so little conversation for so many people, but then again, the afternoon heat on an intercity bus could easily stifle that.

When she reached the three steps descending to the toilet, Laurie paused. For an uncomfortable moment, she thought she was the only female aboard the vehicle, but she felt herself relax, as she looked to the back row of seats where a pretty blonde woman was sleeping on the shoulder of the fat man next to her. He was wearing a loud Hawaiian shirt and gently stroking her hair as she slept. They were sharing iPod headphones.

The toilet was nothing more than a small closet of polished steel. It smelled of antiseptic. Despite the apparent hygienic state, Laurie was a creature of habit, and she used three or four pieces of toilet tissue from the wall mounted dispenser to wipe the lid. Having checked the door was locked, she slid her jeans over her hips and knees, and sat down. As her bladder hissed empty, she stared ahead at metal door, and noticed it was dented in the centre, as if a bull had charged into it.

'Somebody needed real bad,' she muttered.

Laurie finished her business, and reached into the box on the wall to retrieve more tissue. It was then that her fingers met something unusual. Tucked inside the dispenser was a small, folded piece of paper. Laurie's fingers unfurled the crushed note, and realised it had been ripped from a bus receipt, with part of the logo still visible in the bottom corner. The indistinct message on the paper was simple:

My name is Joanne Chapman. I know he's going to kill me. Let anyone know it happened here. Tell Mark I love him, and he was right. 117-565-6315

The words had been written using a flesh coloured pencil – make-up most likely. The writing was oversized and clumsy but the final three numbers were more misshapen suggesting the author had rushed at the end.

Laurie felt her stomach flood with cold adrenaline. She stared intently at the shaky writing, trying to dismiss it. Maybe it was simply a stupid joke. Public bathroom stalls were often defaced with threats and messages. Yet, this message had not been scrawled on the wall; it been hidden, and the rest of the bathroom was clean. Despite the unsettling nature of the discovery, it seemed unlikely to think anyone was murdered in the toilet. Still, something about the note was sinister enough to unsettle her. The word "here" stood out the most.

Standing up, Laurie pulled up her jeans, and she inhaled deeply. As she buttoned her fly, she decided she would get off the bus at Victorville, twenty minutes down the interstate, and contact the police. Whatever had happened deserved to be investigated.

Closing the neat bathroom door behind her, Laurie returned quickly to her seat. Once she had ensured that her bag was untouched, she noticed the curtain had been pulled across the window blotting out the view and the light. She thought it was the creep sitting behind her, trying to get some kind of reaction out of her – or maybe he was a dumb enough to consider it humorous.

However, the elderly man with the book spoke softly. 'I did that.' He nodded to the curtain. 'I hope you don't mind, but the sun was shining on the pages.'

'I'm fine,' Laurie said. *What did it matter now?* She would be getting off in about ten minutes. This meant she would need to contact Vicki, and let her know about the change of plans. Laurie reached into her bag, and produced her phone. It was in that moment a dark line passed in front of her face so quickly it appeared as a momentary blur. She instinctively glanced down at her chest to see a loop of metal appear on her body like a long metal necklace. There was not enough time for her to register what it was, before the brake cable pulled suddenly upwards. Vicki gagged as the metal noose dug into her throat, and she grabbed crazily at the hands squeezing life from her, but they belonged to the man in the seat behind, who simply grunted as he twisted the cable tighter.

Her legs thrashed, and her body bucked, knocking her bag on to the aisle. Laurie's panicky brain held on to the desperate hope the other passengers would stop her attacker, but in her final gasping moments, she saw something that made her thrash all the more. Around her, all of the passengers remained calmly seated. The people in front of her continued staring straight ahead, ignoring her struggle. Directly across from her, the elderly man had put his book upon his knees, and was now smiling at her.

As Laurie fought for her life at the front of the bus, in the back, the large man in the Hawaiian shirt sighed, recovered his earphone from the head of the blonde girl next to him, and let her dead body drop to the floor of the bus.

4

Vicki Reiner was running late, but that was nothing new. In her twenty-three years, it seemed to her that fate ensured she was consistently delayed in life – a fact which had placed her out of step with her fastidiously punctual parents. They would arrive at least half an hour early for any appointment or arrangement. Her mother, who seemed to consider herself above all mortals, liked to state arriving in plenty of time provided a window of additional planning to ensure she was maximising her impact on the world around her.

It was not like that for their daughter. No matter what the day or time, crawling motorhomes, mobile cranes, and flocks of kindergarten children desperate to cross the interstate all seemed to magically appear in front of her car. This happened regardless of the purpose of her journey – she had been tardy for classes, job interviews, and, more recently, therapy sessions. Whenever she complained to her father (who now asked her to call him Steve) in their weekly long-distance phone conversation, he would tell Vicki in an infuriatingly chilled out voice it was simply God's way of keeping her safe. Vicki was not so charitable, and believed it was just God's way of pissing her off.

Still, today she told herself, there was no point getting all stressed out now - after all, she would soon see Laurie, and that created the possibility things would be better again… like they had been before graduation, or, even better, before she had left college entirely.

The previous year had not been a good one for Vicki. She had never been naturally academic, and had slumped beneath the weighty expectations of two professional parents. Through most of her teenage years, she consistently felt her main function was to evoke a heavy air of disappointment in the Reiner household. At the end of each semester, her mother would scrutinize every report card, and interrogate every teacher to identify the cause of her daughter's inexplicable mediocrity.

This was perhaps the reason why, towards the end of her course, she was not even sure that she would graduate. Four years earlier, she had left high school with good enough grades to attend college. This was not testament to her great intellect, but rather because she had always kept her head down and worked as hard as she could. Towards the end of June, she had been delighted to receive an acceptance letter from UC San Diego. The offer related to Computer Science, which appeased her mother mainly because the course had the word "science" in it. But, as graduation grew ever closer, Vicki's father had repeatedly told her this degree might open doors for further avenues of study.

That was, until he got stuck in his mid-life adolescence.

In some superficial ways, college had been easier than high school. The fact most students were, for the most part, on the same intellectual page helped – there was no longer a cluster of hormonal rebels trying to undermine each lesson. But, campus life also seemed to move at a much faster pace than the long, indulgent days of school, and Vicki struggled to keep up. Most of her first year was punctuated by dinner table interrogations from both parents. During her final dinner as a resident of her parent's home, the tension had swelled to a crescendo.

'What did you learn today?' her mother had asked, as she reached across the table for the glass bowl of green salad.

'Mom,' Vicki had laughed nervously. 'I'm not in high school anymore.'

'Honey, I'm only asking because I'm interested,'

'Just looking for an update, Victoria,' her father had said, without looking up from his pasta.

'Well,' Vicki sighed. 'Today, we were looking at file carving. Dad, can you pass the pepper, please.'

'Now.' Her mother had tilted her head, narrowing her eyes. 'You know very well that means nothing to us.'

'Yeah,' her father had nodded, 'sounds like kind of furniture making to me.'

'It's just a way of finding lost data on a computer.'

'Ah, computer forensics.' Her father guessed correctly.

'Yeah, I guess.' Vicki had taken a mouthful of linguine, in the hope of avoiding any further questions. However, her mother would not be derailed so easily.

'So, how did you get on with this *file carving* business, top of the class?'

'It doesn't really work like that,' Vicki had tried to explain. 'It's more like, we all get a drive with hidden data on it, and we have to locate it. There's no scoring against the other students.'

'How do you know how you are doing in relation to the rest of the class?'

'I don't,' Vicki had shrugged. 'But, that's not really relevant to how we work.'

'Work? You see,' her mother said as she turned her attention to her husband, '*that's* what they call further education nowadays.'

'Thanks very much.' Vicki had laid her fork down and sighed.

'Well, it's hardly challenging, is it, if there's no competition.' Her mother had smiled wryly. 'It's more just a play session with computers.'

'Could you do it?' Vicki had raised her eyebrows at her mother, who paused for a moment, as if slapped before regaining her sense of composure.

'I dare say I could.' She had smiled purposefully. 'But, I have more important things to do'

'Important?' Vicki's voice had cracked with emotion, 'like giving masculine jawlines to CEOs, and pouting mouths to bored, rich housewives?'

'Well, those jaw lines and mouths paid for your education, or lack thereof.'

'Come on,' her father said as he held up a calming hand. 'Let's all just…'

'Let's what?' her mother had screeched. 'Pretend that after sixteen years in the education system, our daughter will have a decent career, outside of some grubby little internet café.'

'What more do you want? I did my best at school, even if it wasn't up to your standards. Even after school each day, I accompanied you to your golf club and shooting range, to pursue your interests rather than my own. All the other kids would be at the mall or playing video games, whilst I watched my mother develop her swing or shoot at paper deer shapes.'

'At least those experiences involved some type of skill. Would I have been a better parent if I'd abandoned you in a grubby mall?'

'Okay, I'm done here,' Vicki had said, as she pushed her almost full plate away and stood up.

'Well, I'll put it in the oven, and you can have some later,' her father had murmured, 'when the dust settles.'

Vicki had shaken her head. 'I mean, I'm done living here. I'll speak to the campus accommodation officer in the morning.'

'Well, perhaps that's best,' her mother had said flatly, and turned her attention to cutting her own pasta into perfectly digestible pieces.

As a direct consequence of the final fight with her mother, Vicki had made the move to the campus accommodation at the start of her final year. It was there she found herself sharing a small student apartment with Laurie Ann Taylor. Laurie's first flatmate, a seemingly quiet girl from Iowa, had fallen pregnant, and dropped out of college at the end of the fifth semester. This unforeseen event left Laurie at risk of eviction from the Mitre Court Halls of residence. In desperation, Laurie had hand written thirty-six posters and placed them all conspicuously around the campus.

While Vicki had stood waiting for the bus on the afternoon following the fight with her mother, she had spotted a sign tacked to a nearby door, which read:

Female roommate needed. N/S Compulsive cleaner preferred. No slackers or psychos please.

The poster had featured a row of tear-off phone numbers along the bottom edge. Vicki had ripped one off, neatly folded it in half, and slotted into the card holder of her wallet.

Following a Java Script lecture the following afternoon, Vicki had called the number from a public telephone outside the Behavioural Sciences building. She was both pleased and apprehensive about being invited to view the apartment that afternoon.

As she stepped into the hallway of Mitre Court Hall that day, Vicki had found herself in a stark vestibule, with a row of square post boxes on one wall, and mounted telephones on the other. Directly ahead of her, was a formidable looking glass security door.

Vicki had wandered over to the telephone, picked up the handset, and dialled flat eighty-eight.

'Hi,' a cheery voice had answered. 'Come right up.'

As Vicki replaced the phone, the security door had buzzed angrily. She pushed through it and took the shuddering elevator to the eighth floor.

When the steel door slid open, Vicki had stepped into a long, dimly lit corridor. The air was tinged with a student residency combination of antiseptic and fried garlic.

As she wandered along the hallway, a door up ahead opened, and Laurie had popped her head out.

'Hey, come on in,' Laurie beamed at her.

It was not an expression Vicki was familiar seeing.

Moving into Mitre Court with Laurie was the best decision Vicki had ever made. Spending a year in the company of someone who was so relaxed soothed Vicki's numerous anxieties. Whenever she felt stressed or overwhelmed, Laurie would insist that they head to the beach. She would gather towels and paperbacks, insisting that they let any drama melt away beneath the heat of the sun.

After a day of leisure, once they were suitably relaxed, Laurie would lead Vicki home to sit on the floor eating takeout pizza and formulating a simple plan of action for whatever was concerning her. Compared to Vicki – who had grown up in a luxurious cocoon which left her paralyzed with uncertainty and doubts, Laurie's own bleak upbringing had left her optimistic and proactive. She seemed to possess a knack of breaking any problem into manageable pieces.

As a result of this personal support, Vicki spent the final year of college gaining better results than she ever had previously. She secured a decent degree and felt certain she would finally get the parental approval which had previously eluded her. She was wrong.

On the first Friday after graduation, her parents had taken her out for dinner at a local Thai restaurant, arranged by her father, who fanatically believed Thai food was the healthiest stuff on the planet. This was mainly due to the fact that for his fiftieth birthday, he had attended some Holistic Dentistry retreat down in woods outside San Francisco. He was away for little over a week, during which he made no contact with home. When he had finally returned, Stephen Reiner had taken to wearing an ornate copper bracelet on his wrist, and would regularly bore anyone with his theory, "it's not a theory," he would say, that cumin was the new aspirin.

After they had ordered the food - yellow curry, Pad Thai and fried tofu - her mother had smiled in a disarming manner, before reaching appropriately for Vicki's hand.

'Your father and I are getting a divorce,' she had said, in a deliberately calm manner.

'A what?' Vicki had felt like she'd been punched.

'It's fine, honey.' Her father smiled softly. 'We've been planning it for years.'

Vicki's mother shot him a bitter look.

'What?' He shrugged casually. 'We agreed to tell her, so let's be honest about the whole thing.'

'We haven't been happy for some time,' her mother said, returning her attention to her daughter.

As they were speaking, Vicki had gotten the distinct impression the people sitting with her were pretending to be her parents. As it had transpired, that feeling was not too far from the truth.

Over the course of an uneaten lunch, it was revealed her parents had decided to divorce while their daughter was still in high school. They had also decided this shift in family stability would possibly have a detrimental effect on her education. After some discussion, they had taken the *mature* decision to remain together, if only superficially, until Vicki had graduated from college. The irony was they had taken this bizarre decision in the interest of their child, leaving her unable to criticise their madness, without appearing ungrateful. Their decision, however, had left Vicki utterly debased.

As the fragmented family had left the restaurant that day, Vicki felt all sense of reality melt away. The sun was too bright in the sky above the parking lot. Everything she had known as familiar now seemed untrustworthy and impermanent.

In the months that followed, Vicki had remained in the Oceanside beach house while her mother and father had hastily relocated to the security of their birthplaces in Vegas and San Francisco, respectively. Her parents had mutually agreed they would not sell the beach house on the basis that both parties would share equal access to it. Two weeks after the arrangement was signed, Vicki's mother had the locks changed.

Despite having a nice home in a beautiful part of the country, Vicki felt nothing – not sad or suicidal – just nothing. It was not even the reality of divorce that floored her; it was the simple fact her parents were equally conspicuous in their absence – as if after years of over-involvement in Vicki's life, they had identified graduation as their cut-off point. They had freed themselves from the complication of being parents. Sometimes, Vicki thought perhaps each was assuming the other would take on the burden of main parent. At darker times, she believed she was too dissimilar to both parents to be a worthwhile investment of time, or energy.

Her parents, sensing they had somehow contributed to this, took predictably polarised courses of action. Her mother had sent her several packets of mood lifting pills in long white boxes, while her father paid for a cognitive therapist (possibly even the same one he had used to cope with his mock marriage).

Neither of these methods had made any real impact on Vicki, who grew increasingly detached from the world. She remained living entirely in the beach house, and generated a meagre income from simple web design, and providing online technical support to several businesses. This allowed her to work from home, meaning that maintaining her appearance or mood was not a necessity. Some days, she would lie curled on the balcony, watching the waves for hours, growing lost in the sparkle of the sun shaping and reshaping reality in infinitely changing patterns. The pattern seemed as temporal and shifting as her sense of her past.

In their final support session, the therapist had very calmly suggested it would be *helpful* for Vicki to reconnect with old friends. The idea was not an attractive prospect. Like most people experiencing depression, Vicki felt she had nothing to offer any friend – old or otherwise. She was, in essence, a ghost; disconnected from the bright world around her, and haunting a beach house devoid of the life it had once known.

But, this evening, she had sat and stared at the phone, until she couldn't stand it any longer. So, she had made contact with Laurie, and invited her down to Oceanside. Of course, she had assumed Laurie would have no recollection of her former roommate, or, if she did, might have no interest in travelling for five hours to visit her. She was wrong on both counts. Her friend had sounded genuinely pleased to hear from her, and said she would organise a bus ticket in no time.

During the night, the last thing she had heard from Laurie came in the form of a text message, which arrived just as Vicki was drifting off to sleep. The undulating melody of the cell phone drew her back from the edge of darkness. Her scrambling hand reached for the slim phone in the darkness. Finding the device, she held it aloft in her arm, squinting her eyes against the fierce glow like a lighthouse in the night.

Hi V. bkd amzngly cheap tickt on a Route King bus. Due in 2 terminl at apprximtly 4.30pm. C u thn. xxx

Vicki had smiled to herself when she read the message, and slipped easily into her dreams.

***

The sun was high in the sky, as Vicki eventually reached Victorville Avenue. She pulled off the freeway and parked in the lot behind the bus terminal. Despite the fact that she had arrived in Escondido twenty minutes early, she was now - as always - late.

As she hurried through the terminal doors, she could see the silver bus pulling in to stand twelve. Negotiating her way through the crowd, she kept her eyes eagerly on the bus doors. She was perhaps ten metres away from the vehicle, when the bus slowed to a stop. A smile was already starting to form on Vicki's face in anticipation of seeing her friend.

However, Laurie did not exit the vehicle. The bus stop came to a brief stop - pausing just long enough for an elderly man to step off on to the hot pavement. Almost as soon as the man cleared the bottom step, the pneumatic door hissed shut, and the bus began reversing.

Vicki hurried along the terminal, moving parallel with the vehicle, while craning her neck to see if her friend had fallen asleep, but the tinted windows were too dark to give up their secrets. She called out Laurie's name, but her words were drowned out by the roar of the engine.

Within seconds, the *Route King* bus had rumbled across the oil-stained lot, and moved out into the busy stream of traffic. Vicki anxiously opened her handbag, took out her cell phone, and called Laurie's number. Holding the phone to her ear, she glanced anxiously from side-to-side. Within a couple of seconds, the phone rang. From somewhere nearby, she heard the sound of *"Smoke on the Water"* playing in a looped ringtone. It was the same ringtone her friend had used five years earlier.

Vicki turned around, expecting to see her friend grinning at her. Instead she found herself looking at a strange-eyed young man, who vanished into the crowd. She still held the phone hopefully to her head, but the line died.

5

Oceanside Police Station was housed in an attractive sandstone building. The entrance, hidden between large, peach coloured arches, looked more like the façade of a Mediterranean restaurant than the strategic centre of policing in the San Diego area. However, the cream interior, housing numerous wooden desks and grey metal cabinets, was a busy and highly effective centre of law enforcement.

As he filled up the plain cardboard carton with various items from the bottom drawer of his desk, Detective Leighton Jones found an old photograph. He smiled at the image of a young officer with a gleam in his eyes, as he leaned, arms folded, against a cruiser.

For a moment, the Detective smiled wistfully, before slowly letting the picture fall to his side as he gazed straight ahead into some different time.

Leighton was still two days away from retirement but already felt as if he was fading into obscurity. It was not actually an entirely uncomfortable feeling. After a decade of pursuing murder cases, he was happy to accept the Chief's offer, and slip into normality. Chief Gretsch considered Leighton as a problem – they had crossed swords in the past, and he clearly didn't fit with promotion-hungry new generation of unquestioning officers. Being almost sixty-years-old meant Leighton was neither malleable to fit in, nor young enough to justify a further transfer. Therefore, for the previous two weeks, Leighton had been physically present in the building, but was no longer assigned to any investigations. In some ways, it did make sense. No case would be left unsolved when he left, but it also made Leighton feel like a ghost, as work in the department carried on around him.

Ever since his retirement became common knowledge, his few friendlier colleagues tried their best to rib him with a mixture of humour and affection. Each morning, he would find an item left on his desk. The first had been a brochure for some coastal retirement home. Rather than simply consigning it to the waste paper basket beneath his desk, Leighton put his feet up, and read the brochure from cover to cover, with a wry smile on his face. Each subsequent day brought more "gifts" to his desk – most of them acquired from the lost property storage room. So far, he had found a walking stick, incontinence underwear, two sets of dentures, and several blister packs of Viagra. He had also been given some more appreciated gifts, including half a dozen bottles of dark rum.

For a man who had spent so much of his life working for the Oceanside Police Department, Leighton's job of gradually clearing out his desk and two steel filing cabinets had been depressingly simple. Much of the debris of his career had already been consigned to the trash when the station had moved from a rather serious brick building on Mission Avenue to its new home back in 1999. That transition had been almost as psychologically difficult as his retirement. He had spent most of his career driving to and from that building. For at least six weeks after the relocation, whenever Leighton got a late-night emergency call, he would find himself instinctively driving to the dark and desolate building, before realising his mistake, and turning the car around.

It was 6.15 p.m. as Leighton packed a few more items in the box, before placing his car keys on top of it. Hugging it to his body, he made his way through the building to the car park.

He passed through the report writing area, which was essentially a long rectangular room lined with small wooden booths. Each had its own black swivel chair and laptop computer. However, technology had not quite provided the promised revolution, and Leighton was secretly pleased by the numerous shelves above the booths which were stacked with a variety of report forms and paper documents.

'Good night, Danny,' Leighton said to a young bearded detective, who had a phone cradled to his ear and was typing into a computer. In response to this, Danny twisted around in the chair, and nodded and smiled back at the older Detective.

As he walked towards the exit, Leighton tilted his head in to the dispatch room, where two female workers were moving their attention between a wall of display screens.

'Hey ladies, thanks for the gift, though you really shouldn't have.'

'You're welcome, L.J.,' said Laura, one of the dispatch officers, without looking around from the screens featuring maps and live feeds from car cameras.

The other female, Wendy, glanced around for a second, and gave the Detective a warm smile.

'You all set for the big night out, Jonesy?' she asked with a wink. 'Maybe if the Chief has forgiven you for upstaging him with that Black Mountain Ranch mess, he'll hire you a stripper as a parting gift.'

'Well, I'll be happy, as long as Chief isn't going to be the stripper.'

'I'll drink to that,' Laura said cheerfully.

'Not on duty, of course.' Leighton wagged his finger mockingly.

'Well, you can have one for me tonight,' Wendy grinned.

'The only drink I'll be having is cocoa.'

'Ah, old age does not come alone, L.J.'

'Never a truer word,' Leighton said, with a wave. 'You girls have a quiet night. Remember, if you can't be good, get a decent lawyer.'

All three of them laughed, and Leighton departed, leaving the dispatchers to the busy night ahead.

Leighton had no intention of showing up for his farewell bash. His venue of choice had been an unpretentious bar named Red Rooster over on the Boulevard. Leighton had spent a number of his younger years working in the area as part of the Traffic Division. As a fresh-faced officer with nothing but his TV for company, he had finished many shifts there, consumed his fair share of burgers, and sampled most of the tap beers.

The Rooster was a dive bar, but in a good way, with feisty staff, honest food, and hardworking regulars, who were welcoming to the lonely young officer. More than that, it was a connection to his lost past - when he had first met Heather, and the world had still been good.

On the rare occasions Leighton had stopped in at *The Rooster* – finding the place unchanged through the years - he sat at the bar and felt he had somehow travelled back in time. He would sip at his beer, enjoying the seductive feeling he could step out of the door into the past, and drive home to his previous house on Maple Street, where Heather would be bathing their baby daughter.

In such moments, it was all Leighton could do to stop himself from sobbing into his beer glass. For this reason, the Rooster was more than some random venue; it was a conduit to his lost past, and the only place he would like to raise a glass to the end of his career.

Unfortunately, Chief Gretsch liked to stage-manage all the Oceanside Police station social events – even to the point of arranging uplifting background music - and the Rooster didn't fit with his idea of a good time. He liked to choose a clean venue he could book solely for the event. That way, there would be little risk of his carefully rehearsed speech being interrupted by catcalls from any cynical retired cops or members of the public.

Leighton pushed all thoughts of the party from his mind as he decided to leave the station via reception. Normally detectives would use the staff exit at the rear of the building, but because he was using both hands to carry the carton, Leighton opted for the reception with automatic doors. As he walked towards the front desk, he spotted a girl leaning onto the counter. She was in her twenties and making what looked like an emotional plea to the Janine, the reception officer.

'I'm telling you, I know,' she said, through the hole in the Plexiglas.

'Well, it's probably just anxiety,' Janine said, 'but it I'll take your details, and we can register your friend as a missing person.'

As he passed by the desk en route to the automatic doors, Leighton offered the desk officer a quick smile, and raised an eyebrow knowingly.

It was a warm afternoon and a slight haze from the ocean hung in the air. Leighton liked it like that - finding something clean and optimistic in the quality of the light. Somewhere overhead, a helicopter was droning out towards the sparkling Pacific.

Stepping around to the side of the building, Leighton opened his car, and deposited his box of memories on the passenger seat. He walked around the rear of the vehicle, and climbed into the driver's side. Sliding the key into the ignition, he did not turn on the engine. For a moment, he simply held on to the steering wheel, and stared into the past, as if, in some way, given the right conditions, he could put the car in gear and drive towards it. Despite the light and heat of the day, his internal vision was consumed by a dark, rainy stretch of highway and the bitter stench of burning tyres.

The sound of the sirens in his memory merged with the wail of a cruiser leaving the station behind him. Leighton blinked away the memory, turned on the engine, and rolled smoothly out of the station car park.

It was then, as he turned on to Mission Avenue and was about to accelerate, Leighton noticed the girl from reception. She was sitting on a park bench across from the station, staring at her feet, but her hunched posture told the nearly-retired Detective she felt utterly defeated.

Leighton checked his mirror, pulled his car alongside the kerbside, and got out.

As he walked over the lawn towards the girl, a driver of BMW, who was irritated at the location of Leighton's car, honked his horn, and began shouting abuse at him. Without turning around, Leighton withdrew his badge, and held it backwards. The BMW driver fell silent, and drove off, revving his engine as he went.

'Can I help you, Miss?' Leighton asked from a comfortable distance.

'What?' She blinked, and wiped her eyes in embarrassment.

'My name is Leighton Jones, I'm a detective.' He turned the badge around so she could see it, and moved a tentative step closer to her. 'I overheard you speaking to my colleague at reception.'

'For all the good that did,' the girl sniffed, and rubbed at one eye, smudging her eyeliner into a bruise.

'What's the problem?' Leighton persisted.

'The stupid woman at the desk didn't believe me.'

'Do you mind if I sit down, Miss?'

He took a seat next to the girl, but was careful to maintain a non-threatening distance from her. He could see by her folded arms she was already reluctant to trust him.

'Were you reporting a crime, back there at the desk?'

'Trying to.' The girl wiped again at her smudged eye make-up, and looked wearily at the detective's face.

'I don't know,' the girl shrugged, 'I was supposed to meet my friend yesterday, and she didn't show up.' She leaned forward a bit, and held her face in her hands. 'Have you ever had a feeling something just wasn't right?'

'Many times – comes with the job. So, this friend didn't show up.'

'I know how it sounds,' she sighed, looking at the ground. 'I'm not a total idiot, but something's not right.'

'Look, Miss, it is Miss, isn't it?'

The girl nodded.

'Well, Miss, people go missing all the time. Most of them just have a change of plan, and forget to tell anyone. On occasion, they forget by accident; mostly, it's a choice. Some are runaways, some are lost, but they almost always show up again.'

'This is different.'

'Okay,' Leighton spoke slowly. 'Tell me what happened.' He mentally produced a notepad. It was a visual technique he had used for years. All too often, witnesses would clam up when an investigating officer started writing down details. So he created a strategy to get around this. Instead of a physical pad, he would imagine a black leather notepad, and open it to a clean white page and record the details as he spoke to the witness. Then, in the privacy of his car, he would commit the information to paper.

'I arranged to meet my friend off the bus yesterday afternoon.'

'Yesterday?' Leighton relaxed. In his head, he closed his notepad. There was nothing to worry about in this type of case.

'Who is your friend?' he asked.

'Laurie… Laurie Taylor. She's a college friend, from Barstow – well, from near to Barstow.'

Leighton suppressed a flicker of emotion. Most of the older officers associated the town of Barstow with one of their colleagues, who had raped and murdered a young woman there back in the 1980's. He had been sentenced to ninety years, but died in jail. The association was just a trace memory - nothing more.

'And where were you meant to meet this friend?'

'At the bus station, but she didn't show up,' the woman breathed in shakily, trying to contain her tears. 'And I know that's nothing major, but it's the other stuff that's wrong.'

'What other stuff?' Leighton produced a neat handkerchief and gave it to the girl.

'She told me she had booked a ticket on some new bus company. She was pleased because it was a cheap ticket.'

'How do you know this?'

'She sent a text message to my cell phone.'

'Could she have changed her mind?'

'Maybe, I guess.' The woman's voice took on a doubtful tone.

'Well, have you tried calling her?'

'I did at the bus station. Her phone rang a couple of times, then cut out.'

'Okay. What's your name?'

'Victoria Reiner – Vicki.'

'Well, if I'm honest, Vicki, it all sounds pretty normal to me. You might find that in a couple of days she gets in touch.'

'When I got home, I checked the bus company's website, but it doesn't exist.'

'Maybe your friend made it up. Perhaps she was a bit strapped for cash, and invented the company.'

'But I saw the bus come into the terminal. The doors opened, but she never got off.'

'Could you have been mistaken? I mean, there are hundreds of buses coming through there every hour, and I know from experience a worried mind can get confused.'

'You think I'm being stupid, don't you?'

'No.' Leighton smiled. 'Just being a good friend.'

'It's okay. I'm starting to doubt myself, too.'

'Miss, I'm going to give you a card, with my number on it.' Leighton reached into his jacket pocket, and handed the girl a plain white card, with neat, printed text on both sides.

'That's my office number at the top, and cell phone on the back. If your friend gets in touch in a couple of days' time – as she most probably will – well, then you can just go ahead and toss that card in the trash, but if you still don't hear anything, give me a call.'

'Thank you for this,' Vicki said, as she clasped her hands between her knees. 'I know I could be wrong.'

'Well,' Leighton said, as he stood up, and brushed at nothing on his trouser legs, 'if you're not, we can get this passed on to the Missing and Unidentified Persons Unit, and they can get the ball rolling. Okay?'

'Yeah.'

'You sure?'

'Yeah, thanks, I am,'

'Okay, good day to you, Miss,' Leighton said, with a genuine smile, and turned and walked away.

As he got back into his Ford, Leighton felt a sense of purpose he had not known for many years. It seemed somehow timely one of his final duties as a working police officer would be to help reassure a worried member of the public. He smiled sympathetically at the petty worries of youth, and recalled a quote from Mark Twain about how most of the troubles he had known in his life had never happened.

Pulling back out on to the boulevard, the Detective imagined over the next few days the young woman would finally be reunited with her friend, and perhaps the two of them would laugh over a couple of clinking Mojitos. Maybe the young woman would even speak fondly of the friendly old police officer, who had rightly assured her everything would turn out fine. If that turned out to be the case, then maybe Leighton could finally be the type of person he had always failed to be.

Driving home on that warm afternoon, Leighton pushed a cassette into tape player on the dashboard - it had cost him two hundred dollars to have the CD system removed. The sound of sweet sound of Son House playing *"Delta Blues"* filled the car. Leighton began to drum his hands rhythmically on the wheel. As he sunk into the sanctuary of the music, he was blissfully unaware his cosy vision of the future could not be further from the truth.

6

Anthony Morrelli could not believe his luck. Most weekends he would head to the bar for its 11:00 a.m. opening time, blow his wages far too quickly, and end up getting sent home in a cab before early evening. Tonight, however, he had paced himself and lasted the entire day. Having arrived at Scotty's in the late afternoon, been fed, got drunk, and spent his cab money, he felt a vague sense of accomplishment. With no cash or options, and with the warped wisdom of drunkenness, he decided to stagger unsteadily home along the dark, dusty road leading to town.

Scotty's Bar was a hacienda-style place four miles out of Laughlin, Nevada. It was off the beaten track, but to Anthony, and a cluster of regular patrons, it was worth the journey. The beer was cheap, the waitresses were hot, the burritos were big enough to keep you full for a day and a half, but best of all, none of the asshole tourists ever came out here. Tourists - or fuckheads, as he affectionately liked to call them - were the bane of Anthony's life. His day job down in Laughlin involved renting jet skis and motor boats to idiots who wanted to piss about on the river. Most of them couldn't fit into a life vests or, in some cases, a boat.

"Don't you have anything bigger?" they would whine, day after mind-numbing day. He had even gone as far as buying in a few extra-extra-large personal fucking flotation devices, which resolved part of the problem, but the boats were still designed for reasonably fit people, so he often ended up having to assist, as they squeezed their fat asses in and out of the vessels.

It was a hot night as Anthony wandered along the desolate roadside, and his feet kicked up the dust. Above him, the stars were clear, and an occasional plane would blink a trail towards Vegas. One previous evening, after a day of drinking, he had been walking unsteadily back down to Laughlin, when a neat black triangle had blocked out the stars overhead, as it silently crossed the sky. Anthony had stood with his neck craned watching it, feeling like he was in some Spielberg movie. He imagined for a moment a blinding light would fasten onto his body and spirit him off to another world. But, then, as the angular shape moved away from him, he saw the orange glow of the stealth plane's two afterburners.

He had walked back to town on only one other previous occasion, and that time, he had been accompanied by a guy called Trey Evans. Trey was a small guy and a big drinker. Anthony reckoned he was probably somewhere in his late forties, but it was hard to be sure. He usually sat at the end of the bar, dressed head-to-toe in faded denims, and would often be the last customer there when it closed. Usually, he would be driven back to town by Marianne – one of the more compassionate barmaids. There was nothing romantic about the arrangement – everyone knew Marianne lived in Bullhead City with another woman in a civil partnership. However, one occasion where Trey's hands started to pay her unwanted attention, and another where he vomited on her passenger seat, was enough to end Marianne's generosity. After that, he was required to book a cab, or take the long walk.

The April night Anthony had walked back with Trey had been colder, and they had walked briskly to stay ahead of the frost settling on the desert around them. The fact both men had someone to talk to about baseball, the price of gas, and asshole tourists made the journey pass quickly.

As they reached town at about 3:00 a.m., the men were bonded in drunken accomplishment. They shook hands and agreed they would repeat their journey the following weekend.

But that journey never happened. Anthony had been laid up in bed, after eating some bad prawns, and the furthest he journeyed all weekend was from his bed to the bathroom. The next time he was in Scottie's, he looked for Trey at the end of the bar, but his space was occupied by a group of three women sharing glass jugs of cocktails.

When he asked Marianne if she had seen the small man, she rubbed her temple, and said he'd been in the previous weekend, and made his own way home alone.

Anthony hadn't seen him in the bar in the following months either, and so he figured the journey out of town was perhaps not worth it without the promise of a free ride home.

Shambling through the dark night, Anthony began singing various Bon Jovi songs to cheer himself up. At one point, his tuneless murmur was interrupted by the startling sound of a snake's rattle, coming from the road up ahead. Anthony stopped dead, spreading his fingers on both hands, he looked like a man who had wandered blindly into a field of land-mines. Anthony may have been drunk, but he still knew a bite from a rattler out here, in the middle of nowhere, would mean serious trouble. The creature fell momentarily silent, masking its location. Breathing carefully, Anthony leaned forward, and peered into the gloom. He could see the vague change in tone from the roadside to the sandy scrub, but nothing more than that.

From somewhere in the darkness he heard the rattle, like a crazed maraca. The chilling sound came from somewhere just in front of him, possibly within striking distance. Anthony let out an involuntary yelp, and leapt backwards. His survival instinct overpowered his rational mind, and he ran to the side of the road, then hurried a few metres ahead.

For several minutes, Anthony had walked quickly, imagining if he slowed down, the rattler would somehow catch up with him to take deadly revenge on him for stepping into its hunting ground.

After half an hour of walking at a decreasing pace, Anthony decided walking to town had perhaps not been such a great idea after all. He was ravenous; his feet were hot and sore, with the first sting of a blister on his heel was starting to cut through his drunkenness. He looked over his shoulder in the hope of seeing a car to flag down, but there was nothing except the indistinct grey ribbon of road stretching away from him.

Eventually, a glow on the horizon swelled to reveal an approaching car. A smile crept across Anthony's face, and he began to wave his arms wildly in the direction of the approaching vehicle. In his mind, he was already anticipating getting back home to his trailer, and microwaving some frozen pizza. Not only did the car not slow down, it accelerated and drifted to the opposite side of the road to Anthony.

'Bastard!' he shouted as the tail lights shrank into the distance.

He wandered on for a several more minutes, before the urge to urinate sent him to the edge of the road. He unzipped and sighed as his urine hissed on the arid sand. He shook and zipped up, then began his solitary wander along the deserted road once more. By the time the bus appeared on the horizon, Anthony's attention was lost in a haze of fatigue. He was simply counting his steps in groups of ten. Eventually, the growling engine sound was too loud to ignore.

At first, Anthony thought the low groan was emanating from a 747 rising out of Vegas, but he turned around to see bright lights on the horizon. His next thought was it could be a truck delivering cargo or fuel through the night, but as he peered into the darkness, Anthony Morrelli smiled. It was a bus.

'Well, I'll be damned,' he said. He began to wave his arm back and forwards.

As the bus approached, Anthony held his arm up to his eyes to shield them from the fierce lights. The bus jolted to a stop beside him, and juddered from the vibration of the engine's intestinal rumble. The doors expelled a loud hiss, and slammed open.

Without waiting for an invite, Anthony leapt aboard, and climbed the two steps to face the driver.

The interior of the bus was lit by a cool blue light, in which Anthony Morrelli could discern the vague, dark shapes of sleeping passengers.

'Hi,' smiled the driver, a large man in a Hawaiian shirt. 'You need a lift into town?'

'That'd be great, but hey, I don't have any cash.'

'Don't worry. The meter's not running tonight,' the driver said, as he pulled a lever and closed the door.

Anthony grinned as he staggered along the aisle – from his point of view, his luck was just getting better and better.

7

Leighton Jones was a relatively happy man. He had survived the final week of work with his dignity intact, and was finally getting acquainted with his dwelling. Having spent four days cleaning and de-cluttering, his small apartment was now more like a home than it had been in twenty years. His only stumbling block had been a drawer in the kitchen, where photographs and emotions lay undisturbed, but he promised himself, unconvincingly, he would get around to that whenever he finally felt ready.

However, in the process of tidying his wardrobe, he had dug out a pile of paperbacks he had previously started reading but never finished. They were now stacked neatly on a small table next to the patio door, and it was Leighton's plan to spend each evening after dinner sitting in the setting sun, with a book in one hand, and a glass of iced rum or white wine in the other. There was something fundamentally relaxing about the warm evening air combined with a good book – though, the drink undoubtedly helped, too.

Tonight, he had eaten a small Caesar salad with home-made croutons for dinner, and, having washed up, had moved out on to the patio, where he sat in shorts and a faded denim shirt, with the sleeves rolled up. He took occasional sips from a tall glass of crisp Orvietto, dipping in and out of a Dan Brown novel. This, for Leighton, was as close to contentment as he ever got.

When the car pulled up in front of his small, neatly mown lawn, Leighton glanced absently up from the pages of the book. He took no specific interest in the vehicle; it was amazing how quickly he had slipped off the cop mentality when he had handed in his badge. Not recognising the license plate, he returned his attention to the book in his hand, and did not look up until the shadow of a figure passed over him. Glancing up, he found himself staring at the fresh-faced girl he had spoken to outside the station, three weeks earlier. Her shoulder length hair was tied into a neat ponytail, and she wore jeans with a grey t-shirt.

'Hello again, Detective,' she said. 'I need your help.'

Leighton's mind was momentarily knocked off balance, as he struggled to recall the nature of their previous interaction. He gestured her to sit, and smiled politely.

'What can I do for you, Miss?'

'My friend is *still* missing,' she said matter-of-factly.

'Ah, now, I remember.' Leighton nodded. 'The bus girl, right?'

'Yeah, that's right,' she said flatly. 'The bus girl.'

'Okay.' Leighton took a deep breath. 'Let's start at the beginning. I'm Leighton Jones, and you are Vicki?'

'Yeah, Vicki Reiner.'

'Okay, Miss Reiner. Would you perhaps like something to drink?'

'No, thank you.'

'Well, please take seat. Can you remind me who your friend is, and where she was headed?' Leighton arched his hands into a steeple, and leaned slightly forward.

The girl sat down, but remained rather rigid. 'Her name is Laurie Taylor. She's a college friend, who booked a bus ticket from her home in Barstow to Oceanside - she was coming to stay with me for a while - but she never showed up.'

'Okay, and it's been how long since you last heard from her?'

'Twenty-two days?'

'Are you in contact with any members of her family?'

'No, she only had a mother, who died a few years ago.'

Leighton raised his eyebrows, unsure of the best way to tell this sincere young lady she was most probably wasting both his, and her, time.

'Well, to be honest, look...' Leighton hesitated too long, and the girl's expression hardened.

'I damn well knew it,' she said sourly, and began shaking her head. 'You're still going to tell me to wait.'

'No, I was actually going to tell – '

But, the girl had already reached into her bag, and thrust a number of A4 sheets of paper across the table to Leighton.

'Have a look at this, Detective, then, tell me I'm wrong.'

Picking up the sheets, Leighton looked over the top of them at Vicki. 'What are they?'

'Cell tower records that show the location of Laurie's cell phone. The show which masts the phone pinged off.'

'How did you get these?' he asked curiously.

'Just look at them, please. They begin on August 4th at 1:42 a.m. when an SMS message sent to my phone. After that, she was picked up by the tower at Barstow Station. Then, the Escondido West cell tower picked up her phone, three hours later. Then nothing. No more pings – no more calls.'

'So?'

'So, Detective, from the moment she boarded the bus, Laurie Taylor never used her phone again.'

'And you're certain of that?' Leighton looked at her seriously. 'There can be no other explanation other than she was abducted - no other more likely scenarios?'

'Yes, there are countless scenarios, but I'm certain that something is wrong here.' Vicki held Leighton's gaze.

'Well, I suggest you take these documents along to the Missing Per-'

'I thought we could drive up there,' she said intentionally cutting him off, and brushing absently at nothing on her jeans.

'I beg your pardon?' Leighton put down his glass, and arched his fingers together in front of his chest.

'Yeah.' Vicki grinned. 'The two of us could go take a look at Laurie's place up in Barstow. Well, technically, it's just beyond Barstow, but not much.'

'Miss, may I remind you I am officially a retired police officer, and as such...'

'Exactly, so I know I can trust you.' She grinned at him. 'Plus, since you're retired, you'll also be available during the day.'

Leighton shook his head. 'It's completely out of the question.'

'You said you would help me, that day at the station, and I took you at your word.' She sighed. 'Look, I'll drive, and I'll even buy your lunch. You're retired - it's nice up there - think of it as a day trip.'

'Well, if your friend is missing, what good would it do snooping around?'

'I just thought we could take a look around, see if there's any sign of a break in. You'd know what to look for.' She glanced at Leighton for confirmation of this, but his face gave nothing away. Somewhere nearby, a lawnmower spluttered to life, and the faint smell of cut grass and gasoline fumes drifted by.

'I thought,' Vicki continued, 'if we found something, some kind of evidence, then the police would maybe take the case seriously.'

'Okay.' Leighton tried his best to sound reasonable. 'And if there was no evidence - no fingerprints on the windows, no puddle of blood in the kitchen, or swag bag in the garden, would that be enough to set you free you to move on?'

'I swear.' Vicki held her right hand up, and looked purposely earnest. 'That would be the end of it - you could enjoy your retirement in peace.'

Leighton didn't know if it was the wine, his own loneliness, or the girl's simple tenacity, but eventually, he took a sip from his glass, looked at Vicki Reiner, and nodded.

'Look, Miss Reiner.'

'Vicki.'

'Look, Vicki, I was about to say, before you pushed the paperwork at me, I was never a particularly good cop, anyway.'

'It doesn't matter. I want your help. I trust you.'

'Okay,' he said softly. 'We can drive up tomorrow and have a look.'

'That's great.'

'But,' Leighton held out his hand to quell her delight, 'we take my car and split the gas, and if we find nothing suspicious, you can still buy me lunch, otherwise I'm buying lunch for you, and a little slice of humble pie for me.'

'I knew you were a good man, Detective Jones.' Vicki grinned.

'Or a damn fool.' Leighton chuckled wryly. 'And it's Mr. Jones from now on, Miss. I handed in my badge last Friday, remember?'

'Well, as long as you still have your gun,' Vicki said softly, and got up to leave.

Leighton hoped she was joking, but suspected she wasn't.

After the girl had left, Leighton came in from the patio, and padded through the house to the kitchen. He placed his glass and paperback book beside the empty sink, then pinched the bridge of his nose. For a few moments, he stared at the floor, then slowly turned around, reached down, and opened one of the kitchen drawers. His hand reached tentatively into the back of the drawer, and pulled out a faded polaroid photograph of a seven-year-old girl, affectionately holding a fluffy toy bird. The girl was grinning at the camera, with an expression of delight. Leighton gently stroked the image with his thumb, and peered desperately at the image, as if that small window to the past might somehow open. The tears came quickly, pouring down his cheeks, and dripping on to the black tiled floor. Leighton knew from experience he could not hold back the tide. Eventually, he allowed his legs to bend, lowering himself on to the floor. Holding the picture in one hand, and covering his ashamed face with the other, he wept for hours.

8

nthony Morrelli had closed his eyes as the throaty groan of the engine provided a deep purring lullaby. His eyes were fluttering slightly, as they scanned some imaginary landscape. He was dreaming of his childhood, when his father had taken him fishing for sunfish in the Colorado River out by Davis Dam. It was an activity they had repeated over several summers in Anthony's youth.

Dragging a flaking old boat, with a croaky outboard motor, out on to the steel-coloured river, they would sail west, until they had found a peaceful place to stop. After dropping a couple of dough-bated lines over the side, his dad would open a can of root beer for his son and a bottle of *Peroni* for himself. Then, there was little more than the two of them sitting back in comfortable silence, the stillness broken only by the sound of an occasional fish breaking the surface of the water.

Although he had never analysed it, Morrelli's decision to take up a job on the water four years after his father's death was, in some way, his attempt to reconnect with those lost summers when the warm air blew softly across the gently rocking boat.

Now, seventeen years later, the air was similarly warm, though this time, it was artificially so - drawn in from the cool night, warmed by the heater matrix, and blown through the dark interior of the bus. It swept gently over Anthony Morrelli's cheek, almost as if some soft hand was stroking his face. In his dream, the water was slate-coloured, deep, and mirror still. There was a line trailing out from their boat into infinity. His father was sitting back, silently sucking calmly on one of the ten thousand cigarettes that would eventually kill him - *coffin nails,* he had called them, and they had been. Morrelli always said his old fella's casket should have borne the Marlboro logo.

In the dream, the younger version of himself held on to the fishing line as it grew suddenly taught. He called out to his father in the muted words of dreams, but the man just nodded silently at his son, giving him license to reel in the catch. With the syrupy motion of fantasy, he had reeled in the line, until he saw the vague shape rising up from the depth. Even though undefined in shape, he could tell it was a big one. A smile of pride and pleasure spread across his face; this was no sunfish, more likely a massive pike minnow.

He dragged the resistant beast closer to the surface, and with a final burst of energy, he yanked the creature out of the water and into the boat. But, it wasn't a fish, or even a river crab; it was a massive white spider, with panicky, spindly legs, that skittered against each other, as it pulled crazily at the fishing line tangled around its long fangs. Even in the dream, the rocking motion of the boat seemed terrifyingly real.

The horror of the object pushed Anthony Morrelli up from the slumber of sleep. Although not fully awake, some signals were coming through his dream, merging reality. Despite slipping free of the dream's illusion, the sensation of the wind on his face remained. He opened his bleary eyes to discover someone was stroking his face.

He turned his head to see a small elderly man sitting next to him, touching his cheek. At first, he was confused.

'You have such beautiful skin,' the old man smiled.

'What?'

'Just lovely, golden almost.'

'Old man, if you touch me again,' Anthony said, in a low deep voice, 'I'll break your fucking jaw.'

'So very soft,' the old man continued, almost dreamily himself. He then reached inside his jacket pocket and produced a gleaming hip-flask.

Now, Anthony was suddenly interested, and his scowling expression evolved into something much more amiable. Whatever perversion the old guy subscribed to could be overlooked, for the sake of a free drink.

The small man unscrewed the lid of the flask in a methodical manner, then politely offered it to Anthony. 'Would you like a drink?'

For an unusually perceptive moment, Anthony paused. *What if the old pervert had spiked it?* He glanced around, and realised the bus was almost full of commuters. If the weirdo was dumb enough to try anything, there was an entire bus of upstanding citizens ready to step in. So, Anthony threw caution to the wind.

'What is it?' he asked.

'Wild Turkey,' the old man smiled, and his eyes twinkled.

As the bus hurtled onwards, Anthony grinned, and took the flask from the old man's hand. Tipping the container back, he swallowed three deep gulps of the sweet bourbon, and returned it.

'With a dash of strychnine,' the old man added softly.

'What did you say?'

The old man did not respond. He was too busy reaching across the aisle to access a black Gladstone bag from the opposite seat. When he turned back, he was holding a coil of semi-transparent rubber tubing and an oversized syringe. Anthony, however, was not distressed at the sight of the old taxidermist preparing his tools; he was too busy convulsing and thrashing around in his seat, like someone possessed.

In the cool glow of the blue lights, the old man whistled as he worked. Occasionally, he would call on his fellow passengers to assist by restraining Anthony in his final futile moments, to hold the camera, or to help strip the body. Others would assist by unpacking the plastic sheeting and the large, glass mason jars from the over-head locker.

9

In terms of April weather, the drive up to Barstow was a pleasant one. The sun was warm in the beautiful Californian sky, and the morning haze had burned off to leave the air clear and clean. Leighton had collected Vicki from her beach house – arriving ten minutes early. This was a side of the city Homicide cops rarely visited, and, consequently, he had taken almost half an hour to find Vicki's home in the exclusive beach house complex. Then - afraid of hurrying her too much - he rolled down his window, and sat in the car listening to some Woody Guthrie, until she appeared at the side of his door. She was wearing a faded University of San Diego t-shirt, and had black bandolier bag draped over one shoulder.

'Morning, Detective,' she said, and smiled warmly.

'Good morning, Miss Reiner. You all ready?'

Leighton glimpsed something familiar at her bright eyes, and her long hair pulled back into a loose ponytail. He felt a moment of nostalgia so powerful it threatened to eclipse all other rational thought.

'Raring to go,' Vicki said cheerfully.

'Okay.' Leighton shrugged. 'Put your bag in the back seat, and jump in.'

As Leighton waited for Vicki to get in the passenger side, he gazed at the row of flawless beach houses. They were not the most opulent properties at the beach front, but they still whispered of exclusive wealth. Leighton estimated their value to be somewhere between one and two million dollars apiece.

'Nice home,' he said, as she clicked the buckle shut on her seatbelt.

'Yeah.' Vicki shrugged. 'It used to be.'

Leighton looked at her inquisitively, sensing some shift in her mood. In a moment it had gone, replaced with her smile, and she returned to her previous disposition.

'I just mean, I'm fairly messy,' she said, but Leighton didn't believe her.

Deciding it was better to let the matter drop, he put the car into drive, and they headed off.

They had travelled along the smooth grey interstate for fifteen minutes, before the clamouring traffic spread out, and allowed them both to relax. The car windows were opened just far enough to keep a comfortable breeze of morning air blowing through the interior of the car.

The first thing Vicki had noticed when she stepped into it, was that Leighton's car was immaculate. He had on old style cassette player in the middle of the dashboard; beneath this, was a small shelf, in which a row of plastic cassette cases was carefully arranged in alphabetical order.

'You just had this thing cleaned just for me?' she joked, but Leighton just raised one eyebrow quizzically, and shook his head.

'I just like a tidy car,' he said by way of an explanation.

'Yeah, but there's tidy, then, there's super-tidy.'

Leighton frowned slightly but said nothing.

'Come on,' she pressed. 'This car is clearly too clean - humans need chaos to thrive.'

'What do you want me to say?' he said, feigning irritation.

'You need to explain this - the neat thing.' Vicki laughed.

'It's not a *neat thing*; it's just how I am.'

'Okay,' Vicki nodded in agreement. 'So, where does that neatness come from?'

'Well,' Leighton sighed, and adjusted the rear-view mirror, 'I'm not sure. It just kind of makes sense. For a number of years, my job involved dealing with mess.'

'Mess?' It wasn't really how Vicki had ever considered police work.

'Yeah, you know, messy lives, messy crime scenes, messy desks. I suppose this,' he nodded towards the overly tidy interior of the car, 'is my small place of order.'

He let out a wry chuckle. 'Sometimes, when I'd get called out in the night, my mind would still be groggy by the time I'd arrive at the scene. I'd take a tour of the place, make all the notes I could, and then, I'd go sit in my car. It was kind of like finding a quiet place in the middle of a storm. Some sort of haven, I suppose.'

He paused for a moment, then adjusted his rear-view mirror again. 'I reckon most people could survive just about anything, if they get their own little patch of space, and keep it free from the mess of the outside world.'

'The Leighton Jones mess-free method,' Vicki said resolutely, and smiled at him. 'You could sell that idea and become a millionaire.'

'Amen to that.' Leighton nodded.

Vicki watched, as some unreadable emotion crossed Leighton's face.

'Do you miss it,' Vicki asked, shifting her tone. 'The job, I mean?'

Leighton glanced at her for a moment, then returned his attention to the road. 'I miss some of the people from the station, but no, I don't miss the job in the slightest.'

'But, it must be a good feeling when you solve a murder.'

Leighton said nothing, and his weighty silence was enough to let Vicki know he was unlikely to talk about the job.

They were now heading up through the orchards fringing the free-way north-east of San Bernardino. Vicki gazed out of the window at the neat lines of the orange groves. She wondered how far exactly Laurie had travelled. Perhaps, she had left the bus somewhere out here, and vanished amongst the aromatic trees.

They were driving through Verdemont, when Leighton smiled, and adopted a formal announcer's voice.

'And if you look to your right, ladies and gentleman, you will see a lovely little Pet Cemetery…'

'What, you're kidding, right?' Vicki sat up, and within a few minutes, she saw he was telling the truth. A cheerful sign on the opposite side of the free-way indicated the place where beloved family pets could rest in peace. Vicki smiled at the idea of it, then glanced back at the dashboard of the car.

'You don't have sat-nav?' she asked.

'What?'

'You've driven sixty or so miles, without glancing a road sign?'

'I used to work Traffic before homicide. My job kind of gave me an *internal* compass. I've never really been a big fan of technology.'

'Yeah.' Vicki glanced at his archaic cassettes. 'I get that.'

She looked out of the window again at the sand-coloured hills on the horizon. It seemed like another country in comparison to her ocean view at home. Yet, Vicki thought there was something about the desert landscape that seemed to mirror the sea. It seemed just as vast and unknown.

Turning back to Leighton, she found him looking to the distant horizon, and wondered if this arid world felt like home to him.

'Did you like it out here in open country - amongst the Joshua trees, and lizards?'

'I didn't work this far outside of the city. But I liked taking a drive up here with my kid on my days off.'

'Yeah? So, how come you moved across to homicide?'

Leighton sighed, and shifted in his seat, but said nothing. Up ahead, a couple of motor-homes were playing leapfrog, and slowing down the traffic.

'Well?' Vicki persisted. 'Did you get a speeding ticket, or show up drunk for work?'

Leighton glanced at her quickly, then pinched the bridge of his nose.

'There was nothing scandalous; I just came across a bad accident on the road, one rainy night.'

'Ah.' Vicki nodded. 'A whole lot of fatalities?'

'No, actually, there was just one,' Leighton said, and smiled sadly. 'But, it belonged to my seventeen-year-old daughter. You mind if I put some music on?' His hand clambered over the cassette cases, sending some spilling on to the floor.

'Oh, jeez, I'm sorry. Here, let me help you.'

Vicki carefully gathered the cassettes up, and restored the order. She slotted a tape into the mouth of the player, and the sound of Booker White filled the car, eclipsing any further awkward conversation. For a while, there was nothing but warm road and the hissy old music. Eventually, the tape ended, and the player spat it out in a slow, mechanical manner.

'I'm sorry, Leighton,' Vicki said in the moment of silence, and looked at the floor.

'It's okay,' Leighton said. 'Bad things happen to people every day. I reckon that just happened to be my day. Anyway, this traffic's not going anywhere - must be problems coming in from the Ontario freeway. You fancy a coffee while it settles?' Leighton pointed to a green roadside sign for a diner up ahead.

'Sure.' Vicki, nodded too enthusiastically. 'That sounds really good.'

Leighton drove on to the exit ramp leading to the parking lot of a small café.

The place was busy for a midweek morning. Inside the red brick building, truck drivers and coach trippers occupied most of the booth seats, eating oversized breakfasts of fried food. Vicki offered to pick up their coffees, if Leighton agreed to secure one of the few free picnic tables outside. He accepted, and made his way to the picnic area, picking up a newspaper from the rack en route.

There was a small grassed area at the back of the diner, where a cluster of chunky wooden tables was scattered around haphazardly. Leighton selected a one furthest away from the dull stench of the garbage bins and the screeching chaos of the kiddies play area.

As he sat down, he dragged his hands over his eyes, then looked to the horizon for a moment. To the north-east, he could see the impressive Marshall Peak against the hazy blue sky. He had managed to avoid driving around this area for several years, but now he was back, as if summoned by his private ghosts. He wondered if he was doing the right thing, agreeing to a trip back to his past, especially with a young woman. But, before he could arrive at any conclusion, a shadow passed over him.

'Here you go.' Vicki smiled, as she carried the brown tray of coffee and pastries to the table where Leighton was sitting, peering at the horizon.

'Let me help you,' he said, as he stood awkwardly.

'It's okay,' she said, placing the tray down. Vicki then sat, and handed a crinkled paper coffee cup to Leighton.

'I know you said you didn't want anything, but I'd feel bad eating a Danish in front of you, so I got two almond croissants, oh, and two cinnamon whirls.'

'Vicki, that's very kind of you, but four?'

'Yep, it was buy one get one free.'

'Hmm.' Leighton looked unconvinced, but he accepted a pastry gracefully and sipped his coffee. The girl seemed calmer than she had been during their previous encounter, but he was unsure of what was really going on behind her frequent smiles. If, as he suspected, she was desperately obsessing about the unlikely disappearance of her friend, it was probably because something was missing elsewhere in her life. God only knew, following the loss of his daughter, Leighton had clung on to enough things himself.

'So,' he said softly, 'about today?'

'What about it?' Vicki tore off a fluffy piece of croissant and popped it in her mouth.

'Well, how are you feeling?'

It was now Vicki who looked to the distance for a moment, then turned back to meet Leighton's gaze.

'Excited, or something close it, I suppose.' She exhaled. 'Though, I don't know if *excited* the right word for this experience.'

'Why?'

'Well, either way, I'll get closer to knowing the truth - we find some sign of a break in, and so have something to go to the police with, or we find Laurie hiding in her hometown, just trying to avoid her unstable old college buddy.'

Leighton took a bite of his pastry, washing it down with some coffee, and looking across at Vicki.

'But, you really don't expect to find her there, do you?' Leighton sipped his coffee again, but held Vicki's gaze.

'No,' Vicki said conclusively, and turned her coffee cup around absently. 'I don't.'

'Though, you do accept it is possible,' he said tentatively.

'I guess so.' Vicki shrugged.

'You see, I think, in life, it's better to assume the simplest explanation, until you are presented with evidence to the contrary.'

'But, I have evidence to the contrary.' It was Vicki's turn to hold Leighton's gaze.

'You have what a court would consider *circumstantial evidence.*'

'But, people have gone to jail based on less,' Vicki responded, her tone more challenging.

'That's true.' Leighton nodded. 'But, most don't.'

'I showed you the phone records. Why would someone suddenly stop using their phone?'

'Because it was broken, or lost, or stolen - any number of reasons.'

'Jeez, I hope I never drop off the radar, and have to rely on Oceanside Police to locate me.'

Leighton chuckled and took another drink.

'Oceanside PD does a fine job,' he said. 'Part of which is discerning whether or not a crime has actually been committed.'

'Well, Detective - sorry, *former* Detective - what is your professional opinion, based on the evidence, circumstantial, or otherwise?'

'Let's consider what we have…' He held his hands out to her, palms upturned.

Vick nodded encouragingly.

'There was once this girl, who, out of the blue, received an invitation from an old college friend, which she apparently accepted.'

'Okay,' Vicki agreed in grudging approval.

'And - assuming she actually did accept the invitation - maybe this girl went as far as taking the bus trip down to meet her old friend. Only, at some point, she realised she couldn't really afford the trip, or maybe, an old boyfriend or a different friend called up and gave her a better offer. So, feeling embarrassed, she stupidly gets off the bus, before it ever reaches the bus station, probably somewhere like this.'

'But, I heard her phone ring in the station.'

'Or - more specifically - you heard *a* phone ring. Even if it was exactly the same ring tone as your friend had, that is hardly beyond coincidence.'

'So, how do you explain the fact it was picked up by the cell phone tower in Oceanside?'

Leighton looked at Vicki, gauging how to explain the possible events, without hurting her feelings. 'It is quite possible she left on the bus intentionally, to avoid any difficult conversation. You did say it didn't register any more calls.'

'She'd deliberately lose her own phone?' Vicki looked at him, incredulous.

'Yes, that way, if she finally does get back in touch with you, she can justify her silence - the lost phone. That would explain why she missed your calls and lost your number. If you accept that, isn't it also possible after Laurie got off the bus, somebody picked up her shiny phone?'

'I suppose.'

'Therefore,' Leighton said sagely, 'even if you did hear it at the bus depot, it is not necessarily evidence of anything suspicious.'

The former detective took a drink of coffee, then arched his hands together in front of his face. He felt confident he had addressed Vicki's concerns, but then, she threw him a curve-ball.

'So, how do you explain the fact she hasn't shown up for work in the last week?'

This seemed to catch Leighton off-guard. His eyes widened slightly, and his mouth opened just a fraction, but he quickly regained his composure.

'Maybe she planned to stay with you longer, and so left work with no definite plan to return.'

'She took two weeks of annual holiday – that's all she was entitled to – and she hasn't been back, even though it was payday last Friday and she has wages to collect.'

'You know that for certain?'

Vicki nodded resolutely. 'I called and spoke to the owner, he told me that he had already replaced her. Missing waitresses don't clear tables.'

Leighton drunk his coffee and smiled. 'There could be a number of reasons for her avoiding work too, but I guess whatever the truth is, we'll be better placed to find out when we get to Barstow.'

10

Mark Steinberg had suspected something was wrong after two or three days, but after five weeks, he was almost certain. As free spirited as she was, Jo would have been in touch. He had told her several times he would accompany her down to Santa Cruz, if she would just hang on for a few more weeks. He had some holiday time due from work, but Jo was unable to hang around; she simply wanted to get playing some gigs, and The Black Cat club in Santa Cruz seemed like the perfect venue. And even though it hurt Mark to admit it, Santa Cruz probably also represented freedom.

The previous December, he had been working at the Sundowner Bar in Laughlin – it was a grubby little bar, on the edge of town. It had been in a slow decline for years, until Mark and another barman organised regular live music evenings. Initially, it had been a relatively slow burn, but by the third month, and having slashed beer prices during any performance, the bar began to gain a reputation as a credible little venue.

Jo had shown up for a Sunday night open mic session. With her rebel prom queen looks, she seemed like out of place, as she dragged her battered guitar case through the door. She approached the counter and confidently parked herself on a stool facing the tiny raised stage. She ordered a bottle of European beer, and, as she drank it, she tucked her hair behind one ear. This action revealed a neatly scripted tattoo beneath her ear which read: *Sorry is so easy to tell, yet so hard to express.*

Mark, who had been working behind the bar on the night she came in, had been down in the cramped cellar changing a barrel of Anchor Steam. He had volunteered to go down to escape the earnest teenager, who was murdering a selection of Simon and Garfunkel songs. When he climbed back up through the hatch in the floor, and saw Jo at the bar, he forgot all about the terrible music. She looked like she had been transported from a time when beauty was natural, and fashion was simple. He straightened his faded Ramones t-shirt, and, picking up a bar towel, moved over to where she sat.

'Hey, is this your first time in here?' he said, trying to sound casual, as he wiped the counter.

'Yep,' she said, as she kept her eyes on the singer.

'So, what do you think?' he persisted.

'Seems an okay place.' Jo said, and drank her beer.

'Just okay?' He assumed an expression of mock indignation.

'Yep,'

'Ah well, hey, listen, the entertainment is usually better than this.'

'He's not so bad,' she said, without turning around.

'Really?'

Mark waggled his eyebrows, causing Jo to giggle.

'Well, I've heard worse.' She glanced at Mark. '... but only rarely.'

'You play and sing?' Mark nodded towards the guitar case.

'Yep, when I unpack this bad baby,' she patted the guitar case, 'I'll knock your socks off.'

Jo had not been lying, either. That night she had patiently waited until the local singers had performed their tired sets, before she unpacked her guitar, and stepped up on to the stage.

'Hi,' she said, into the grubby microphone, 'this is a lovely Marianne Faithful song for the lovely barman.'

While Mark watched in appreciative silence, Jo played a powerful version of "Ruby Tuesday." She strummed and picked the strings with skill and style, her head tilted to the single spotlight, as she sang her heart out. The first song was followed by a couple of Cat Stevens and Lou Reed numbers. For the first time in months, the entire audience of the small venue were wholly engrossed in the performance of a stunningly good musician.

Once Jo had finished her set, she sat at the bar with Mark until closing time. She had explained she was originally from Boulder City, and after quitting her job in a dead-end shoe shop, had decided to gig her way down to the West Coast. The idea of hopping from bus to bus, and busking down to San Diego, appealed to her sense of connection with the romantic past.

Mark, who shared her fascination with the music of the past, felt he had found a kindred spirit, especially when Jo's face lit up in discovering he spent daylight hours working in a retro record store over on the east side of the city.

After the bar closed that night, Mark walked Jo back to her motel. He had carried her guitar, and she had held on to his arm - like Suze Rotolo - as they made their way through the deserted town. After raiding the mini bar of its only two drinks, they had sat on the balcony, and raised two miniature bottles of Jim Beam bourbon in a toast to the bright stars above them. Then, they had slept together on the soft bed, where their lips and hands had moved over each other in the warm darkness.

That had been the start of three and a half blissful months. During the day, Mark worked in RPM Records, and Jo wrote new songs on her battered guitar. At lunchtime, she would show up at the shop with paper bags of home-made sandwiches and clinking bottles of root beer. They would have a daily picnic on the floor of the stock room, surrounded by stacks of vinyl albums, where they would debate Dylan's move from acoustic to electric guitar, or the decline in modern lyrics.

In the evening, they would spend their time in the bar, gradually building up the quality and reputation of the music nights.

Eventually, inevitably, Jo grew restless to continue her journey. She would talk about the West Coast more often - usually in terms of 'when' rather than 'if' she would get there. She had been digging around on the internet, and wanted to play in a popular music venue called The Black Cat bar.

It had been tough for Mark, who had found everything he ever wanted in Jo, to know she was still looking for something more. But, he was wise enough to know she was like a wild bird - stuck in a cage, and dreaming of wide blue skies. She talked as if getting down to the Coast would be a visit, but they both suspected otherwise.

As the lay together in bed one night, with Jo facing the bedroom window, Mark asked the difficult question.

'Do you want me to drive you down, just from a safety point of view, I mean? I have some time off coming up. No strings.'

'It's okay,' she said softly.

'I don't mean in a stalker "take me with you" way. I just meant to save you taking the bus.'

'It's okay.' Jo half turned and smiled. 'I kind of like the old bone shaker buses, plus I got a really cheap ticket - all the way to San Diego for fifty bucks. Leaves tomorrow night'

'Oh.' Mark took a deep breath. 'Sorry, I didn't think you'd booked already. Are things here that bad?'

He sat up in bed, took a cigarette from the night stand, and lit it.

'Mark, I'm not trying to get away from you,' Jo said, as she turned fully around, and placed a hand on his arm, touching the edge of a spiralling tattoo. 'I'm just trying to find my place.'

'I know,' he said, blowing out a cone of smoke. He knew this was true. 'Look, Jo, I'm not trying to be some ball and chain. Whatever you need to do is cool. But, I'm not naïve - you have the heart of a poet, the voice of an angel, so I'm guessing you might not be showing up here again too soon.'

'Never say never.' She shrugged. 'Plus, you could always come down, too.'

He shook his head. 'I wouldn't want to be your baggage.'

'Then, how about a weekend trip?'

'Maybe once you're settled, eh?'

'Yeah, that would be nice.'

She turned away and Mark switched of the night light. The sound of The Blue Oyster Cult was drifting through from the living room. Somehow, the darkness made it seem louder.

As he pressed against her back, Mark slipped a hand on to Jo's warm stomach, and closed his eyes.

'I do love you,' he said, his mouth against her warm soft, shoulder, but she was already away.

That had been the last night he ever spent with her.

The following evening, Mark drove Jo to a bus stop on the outskirts of town. They had sat and waited in the car, until the silence was unbearable for both of them. Then, they had stood uncomfortably apart by the roadside, until the silver coloured bus had arrived. The driver - a large, friendly guy in a Hawaiian shirt - loaded Jo's guitar case into the luggage compartment, as Mark gave her a quick hug, and said his brief goodbye. He watched the tail lights of the coach shrink into the darkening horizon, feeling like he had been robbed.

Now, five weeks later, he sat alone in his apartment, and rubbed his hands over his unshaven face. If she had been in touch, then, he had been prepared to move down to the Coast for a few weeks. They could see how things went, and simply chill out for a while. But, as time passed, Jo had not contacted him - no phone call, no email - just a void. It seemed to Mark she was either sending him a message she was happy without him, or something had gone badly wrong.

Despite the pain it caused him, Mark hoped the reason was the former, but somewhere at the back of his mind, a small alarm bell was ringing.

11

The town of Barstow was slightly larger than Vicki had expected. The way Laurie had spoken about it made it sound like one dusty street in the middle of the desert. Instead, it was a cross of intersecting roads, which formed a basic grid of functional homes and single storey businesses.

Leighton turned the car into the parking lot of Barstow Station. 'Okay, this is the town,' he said, 'so what's the address?'

'4 Vineyard Drive,' Vicki said. She was holding a home printed map in her hand, but didn't need to consult it.

'If you drive through the main street, keep going until you leave the built-up section, you'll reach Burke's End, then turn right, then left - it's the fourth house along. They are fairly spread out.'

'I thought you said you had never been here?' Leighton said, as he put the car in gear, and began driving back out on to the street.

'I haven't,' Vicki confirmed. 'I checked out the town online a few times. I must've just learned it by osmosis.'

Leighton shot her a sceptical glance. 'Maybe you should consider a career with the Oceanside Traffic Unit,' he said wryly.

'I doubt I'd be very good,' Vicki said softly.

'You couldn't be any worse than I was.' Leighton's words could have been taken as a joke, but there was no humour in his voice.

It took no more than a few minutes for Vicki and Leighton to travel along the dusty road leading through the Burke's End area to Laurie's home.

As the car pulled into the roadside, Vicki suddenly felt a sick feeling form in the depth of her stomach. Up until that moment, she had somehow managed to push the reality of the situation to some dark area of her mind. But, now, she was forced to confront the painful truth.

Looking at the single level, misshapen bungalow, with peeling rust coloured paint and colourless felt roof, made her guiltily aware of the extreme contrast between her own Oceanside accommodation and Laurie's humble home. This sad fact seemed to solidify Vicki's commitment to finding her friend.

'You coming?' Leighton smiled briefly, and unclipped his seatbelt, but his tone had become business like. Crime scenes - if this was indeed one - were as familiar to him as his own home.

'Sure.' Vicki nodded, as if to motivate herself, 'Let's go.'

Vicki opened the creaking car door, and stepped out into the dry heat. Laurie's house sat on an empty stretch of desert road. Directly across the street from the small house was a weed-covered pile of sandstone rubble, which may once have been a similar building, but other than that, Laurie's home looked out on nothing but flat, dusty fields filled with needle grass and giant cardons poking up like prickly scarecrows.

Even to Leighton, it looked like a lifeless and lonely place to live.

Vicki imagined what it must have been like for Laurie, who had dreamed of leaving college to take photographs in Europe, to have found herself stuck in a shack on the edge of a desert town.

The front garden of the grubby house was little more than four square metres of dead grass ringed by a waist-high fence of sun-bleached wood. Leighton lifted the loop of green garden wire, which held the small wooden gate shut, and pushed it open.

'After you,' he said, and stepped aside to allow Vicki to approach the house first.

Vicki stepped cautiously towards the hazy screen door at the side of the building. She almost tripped over a swollen bag of trash, which sat surrounded by a scattering of crushed cigarette stubs. A cluster of house flies buzzed in the air around the garbage, as if to protect their territory. Vicki wondered how many of their wriggling offspring were feasting inside the plastic bag.

Turning her head back, she found Leighton was peering intently at the rust coloured soil beneath the windows.

'Should I try the door?' she called.

'Sure,' he responded, without looking up.

Vicki reached towards the steel door handle then hesitated. 'Hey, what if they need to, you know…'

'What?' Leighton called.

'I don't know.' She searched for the right words. 'Maybe check for prints later?'

'They can discount yours,' said Leighton, who was crouched near the ground, peering at the garden gate. 'I'll vouch for you.'

'Okay,' Vicki nodded, 'sure.'

As she reached for the handle again, Vicki closed her eyes, and silently wished for the impossible. She wished the door would open easily, and inside, she would find Laurie sipping a glass of iced tea, and wearing one of her trademark outfits, listening to classic rock. Her mouth would fall open at seeing her friend. She would laugh, rush to hug Vicki, and explain she had somehow gotten all mixed up. Perhaps she would even invite the strange old detective inside to have a drink with them, and share in the joke. But, that was not going to happen, because when Vicki opened her eyes and held the handle, she found that the door was locked.

'Any luck?' Leighton said from directly behind her, making her jump.

'Shit!' Vicki let out a deep sigh.

'Sorry, I thought you heard me talking to you as I came along.'

'No, it's okay, but I never heard you.'

'I was saying there's no sign of a break-in at the front of the place.'

'Well, this door is locked, too.'

'Then, let's have a look around back.'

Leighton walked around to the rear of the property to find nothing more than a fence, a patch of parched grass, and a grey plastic bird feeder. Vicki followed him but said nothing. The retired detective turned his attention to the house. The rear wall of the property had one small window and a glazed sliding door. He walked over to the door and crouched down. After a moment, he walked to the window, and put his face close to the glass, peering at the lower corners.

'You think someone could've broken in through there?' Vicki asked.

'No.' Leighton shook his head. 'The window's too small to get through.'

'So, what are you doing?'

'I'm just making sure there isn't a body in here.'

'Oh.' Vicki felt a momentary jolt of fear. 'But, you can't see inside.'

'Come over here a second.' Leighton beckoned to her.

Vicki walked cautiously over to where Leighton stood.

'Look in through the glass,' he said, his voice deep and reassuring.

Vicki stood on her tiptoes, and cupped her hands over her eyes to reduce the glare of the sun. Leighton was close enough so that Vicki could smell his faint cologne - musky and sweet.

'What can you see?' he asked.

'Nothing really - the blind is down, and there's just a tiny space at the side of it.'

'What if you look down?'

Vicki cast her eyes downward. 'Just the window ledge.'

'Anything on it?'

'Yeah, a small white ashtray, with some nickels and dimes in it?'

'But, that's all you can see on there?'

'Yeah.' Vicki pulled back from the glass and turned to Leighton. 'Didn't tell me much.'

'If your friend was in there, even just because of an accident - carbon monoxide, a slippery bathtub or faulty electrics say - well, after two or three weeks, that window ledge would be covered in flies. In summer like this, they can fill a house in a fortnight. I also checked the windows at the front and side, they're clean, too.

All of the main access points into the property are secured and undisturbed.'

'What does that mean?'

'I believe it means you are going to buy me lunch.'

Vicki fixed him with a surprised expression, though not entirely shocked by his comment.

'It's okay.' Leighton smiled. 'Now we know her home is secure, we can discuss where Laurie is most likely to be, but we do it over some food, okay?'

'Okay.' Vicki sighed and smiled. 'Let's go, Sherlock.'

They walked back to the car, and climbed inside. It was just as Leighton had started to drive along the road Vicki grabbed his arm to stop him.

'Oh shit! Hang on,'

The car lurched to a stop.

'What's wrong?' Leighton asked, as he applied the parking brake.

'I left my bag in the yard, hang on,' she said, as she unclipped her seat belt, and clambered out of the car.

'I'll wait,' Leighton said, 'but the meter is running.'

Sighing, he picked up a bundle of tape cassettes and began choosing his next play list. A few moments later, Vicki climbed back into the passenger seat, clutching her bag to her chest. Leighton noticed she was breathing hard, too, with a mist of spray on her forehead.

'Bit stressed. Thought you'd lost it, huh?' Leighton said, as he restarted the engine.

'Yeah.' Vicki nodded. 'My backpack is my life.'

'Amen to that,' he said, and the car rolled along the dusty track towards the centre of town.

12

As he lay on the ground, with his hot urine soaking through his shirt, California Highway Patrol Officer Charlie Thomson marvelled at how quickly circumstances could change. Nineteen minutes earlier, he had been cruising along Route 138, where the freeway cut through the San Bernardino National Forest.

Around that time, he had felt the first grumbling of hunger starting to form in his gut, and was thinking about a stopping off at the Lazy Faire Ranch for a burger. The place was only a few miles down the road, and the traffic was light for a weekday, so Charlie was confident he could get there less than in ten minutes.

The afternoon was warm and bright. Charlie had eased off the gas as he approached a curve in the road. It was then that he noticed the sunlight glinting off something reflective located within the trees at the roadside.

Slowing down the bike, he turned his head to get a better look, and realised something large and silver was sitting partially concealed by the fringe of trees bordering the highway. Charlie pulled into a lay-by and, after waiting for a stream of cars to pass, turned his bike around and crossed over on to the north bound side.

As he cruised slowly along the highway running parallel to the treeline, Charlie could clearly see shiny metal panels. As an officer with six years' experience, he knew there was no designated parking this far north in the park. It therefore seemed likely the vehicle was possibly stolen, then abandoned. He slowed the bike to a smooth stop on the verge of the road. Kicking down the stand, he climbed off his bike, and unclipped his helmet in a single practised move.

As he walked towards the trees, the officer glimpsed more metal from the object set back into the woods. Initially, he had thought it might be a food van, or even an old style polished RV, but stepping through the shadowy trees, he could see the actual size of the vehicle, which appeared large enough to be a truck trailer. He stumbled on a gnarled root and had to grab on to a tree for support. Although he was only moving twenty or so metres away from the freeway, Charlie noticed how eerily quiet the area was – as if someone had turned down the volume on the cosmic remote.

By the time he had walked several more metres towards the vehicle, Charlie realised there was no bird sounds either, just the regular sound of his own breathing. For some reason, he found himself thinking of the "Teddy Bears' Picnic" song - it slipped into his head, and occupied the void left by the departing sounds of the world.

Leaving the treeline, Charlie stepped into a rough clearing, and paused in confusion before a large old fashioned bus. This was not something which belonged in the middle of the woods. The bulk of the body of the vehicle was a dull silver colour, and the windows were dark and grimy. The officer figured it had been the sun glinting off the metal panels which had initially snared his attention. Still, it was strange to find something like this in the middle of nowhere. There was no actual road here; it looked like the bus had simply dropped from the heavens, or been pushed up from below.

Charlie's eyes narrowed as he peered beneath the bus. The weeds sticking out of the dry earth appeared to be green and healthy, suggesting the bus had only arrived there recently. He stood up and gazed around at the ground and bushes. The immediate vicinity looked as if a cluster of vehicles had recently been parked nearby. Moving cautiously closer to the bus, the officer's right hand instinctively found the solid comfort of his Smith and Wesson. He slid along the side of the bus, and reached the open door. Darting his head around to glance through the opening, he found the drivers' seat was empty. Most likely whoever had dumped the bus here was long gone.

'Hello?' he called out. 'Police. Is anyone aboard the vehicle?'
There was no reply.

Holding his gun before him like torch, Charlie Thomson boarded the bus.

Stepping up into the silence of the vehicle, the officer noticed an unusual smell that didn't seem to fit with public transport, but a hospital or dental surgery - clean and antiseptic. He moved slowly along the central aisle, suppressing the urge to run his hands along the headrests. A sweep of the bus revealed it was not only empty, but utterly spotless. This fact struck Charlie as seriously weird. He had been on numerous buses in his life, but none of them looked like you could eat your dinner off the floor.

As he stepped off the bus and into the bright sunlight, Charlie decided the best way to deal with the situation was to radio it in, and get a team out here to investigate the scene. The technicians could use their tape and tubes, and Charlie could sit down for lunch. Turning his head to one side, he brought his hand up to the chest-mounted radio and paused. There was something wrong beneath his feet. It was the combination of sound and texture that drew his attention. Staring down at his feet, he realised he was standing on a wide square of clear plastic sheeting. This was something that had definitely not been there before he boarded the bus.

Before he had time to process the terrible implication of this shift in his environment, Charlie Thomson felt a sharp wasp-like sting on the left side of his neck. His hand shot up to the site of the pain, where his fingers found the small source of his discomfort. Pulling the foreign body from his flesh, he stared at it, and momentarily thought it was some type of insect. But, as he brought his hand closer to his face, Charlie found himself staring at a steel dart, with an orange furry tail. Before he had time to process this development, his right leg suddenly buckled beneath him, and Charlie felt himself collapse on to the slick plastic sheeting.

The material felt strange against his sweating face, and smelled faintly chemical. As he tried to move his limbs, the police officer felt his energy drain away, leaving him face down in an unnatural position. In the dreamy haze of the paralytic agent, Charlie was vaguely aware of a figure walking towards him. He tried to turn his face around to get a clearer view, perhaps see a face, but by then, the paralysis was complete. All that he could see was a pair of work pants, the bottom half of a Hawaiian shirt, and the dull grey metal of a tranquilliser gun.

'Hey there, Snoopy,' a voice said quietly. 'I think you were sniffing around 'cause you wanted a ride on my bus. Well, okay, let's get on, and see where it's heading.'

13

The inside of the car felt sweltering to Vicki as she closed the door. The car turned out of the dusty track and onto a real road. It had taken a moment for the groaning air conditioning to kick in. During this time, Vicki's eyes had remained fastened on the reflection of the ramshackle house fading away in the wing mirror. However, once they had turned off, it was lost from sight ... much like the owner.

'So, where do you want to eat?' Leighton asked, as he pulled on his seat belt.

'Huh?' Vicki shifted from being lost in the past.

'I asked, where you wanted to go for lunch.'

'Well,' Vicki pretended she was thinking, 'how about we visit The Palm Café?'

'Is that where Laurie worked?'

'Ah.' Vicki smiled. 'Now somebody's back in detective mode. Yeah, it's where she worked. It's just off the main drag, back in Barstow.'

Following Vicki's directions, Leighton drove the car along a business loop of Route 15, and pulled into a small parking lot covered with a patchwork of tarmac. The midday heat was heavy and unrelenting, as the young woman and older man left the coolness of the car to cross the hot grey expanse. Vicki struggled to shake of the strange numbness of the sense of loss she felt.

Inside The Palm Café, Vicki and Leighton found a seat next to the window, but thankfully out of the scorching sunlight. They ordered a couple of burritos – vegetable for Vicki; chicken for Leighton - and two iced teas. The two members of staff, who were mopping the red tiled floor and serving the food respectively, were cheerful, and the place was bright and airy, but the view from their table was of little more than the Nu-Way car wash and, beyond that, Soutar's Ford Dealership.

'So.' Vicki smiled. 'We must stop meeting like this.'

'Yeah.' Leighton glanced around. 'We could write a travel guide to the fast food joints of North America.'

'Somebody would buy it.' Vicki shrugged then added, 'Possibly.'

'Is the town what you expected?' Leighton asked, as he undid the cuff buttons of his pale blue shirt.

'I suppose it is … kind of. A bit hotter and dustier.'

'Well, once you head inland from the coast, this is what you get. Have you only ever lived by the water down in Oceanside?'

'Yeah, but not always at the beach. We used to live in a house over on the west side, in Parkland Heights.'

Vicki saw by the slight arching of one of Leighton's eyebrows he knew of the exclusive area and the ridiculous price of the homes located there.

'Yeah, I know. My father is a cosmetic dentist, and my mother is a maxillofacial surgeon, so they pulled in the dollars.'

'How come you moved from there?' Leighton asked.

'After the divorce, my father moved into the beach house for a time, and I spent most of my time down there. That suited me; I always preferred that place to my mother's palace. Anyway, eventually, when my father moved down to San Francisco, my mother sold the big house.'

'It must have been hard, leaving your home, and coping with divorce.'

'I guess. To be honest, I never really thought of the place in Parkland Heights as home. It was too clinical and so large it felt almost empty. Even the gardens up there all have high walls, like prisons. You never see or hear any of the neighbours. Living there was like being a princess in a big empty palace. It probably sounds really messed up, but when I was looking at Laurie's little place back there, I was thinking how more like a real home it seemed.'

'Well,' Leighton smiled, 'the other side of the tracks always looks more appealing than the one you're on.'

'I know, and I like the beach house best of all – that's where I got to be a regular kid. But, it's still on loan from my mother.'

'She charges you?' Leighton's eyes widened.

'Not exactly. Despite spending most of her time in New York, she wanted to keep the beach house for her retirement. She couldn't stand the idea of renting it out to strangers who would – and I quote "*contaminate the place*". So, she told me I could live there rent free and maintain the place, but only on the basis I change none of the décor, and use the alarm system on a daily basis.'

'Seems very practical.' Leighton smiled sympathetically.

'That's my mother for you.'

The conversation was halted by the arrival of a waitress, carrying a tray to their table.

When the food had been placed before them, Vicki and Leighton ate in comfortable silence. To any onlooker, they might have appeared to be a father and daughter, who had not seen each other for a while, and were breaking the ice with some fast food.

Once they finished their meal, Leighton excused himself to use the bathroom, but stopped on the way to speak to a senior waitress, who was setting up a table for a kid's party. As he moved away from the table, Vicki reached into her bag, and removed a neat tablet computer, which she switched on, and began typing furiously.

When Leighton returned, he found Vicki frowning intently at the small screen.

'You brought a computer?'

'No.' Vicki carried on, typing intensely.

'You found a computer?'

'No, it's not mine; it belongs to Laurie.'

'Where did it come from?' Leighton frowned.

'Her bedside table.'

'You broke into her house?' Leighton shook his head in disbelief but remained standing.

'Not exactly, she always keeps a key under her door mat. I didn't break anything.'

'But, you entered the property, and removed that item?'

'Yep,' Vicki said, as she typed.

'You realise you've committed a crime, and if your friend is in any kind of trouble, you've contaminated a crime scene?'

'You told me there was no *crime,* therefore it couldn't be a crime scene.'

Leighton ran a hand through his hair and sighed. 'This was what you wanted all along?' he asked.

'Yep.' Vicki continued typing.

'So, why involve me at all? Why drag me one hundred and fifty miles away from home, when you could have shown up, broken in, and stole the laptop yourself?'

'I needed you as a witness to prove I'm not a thief. Plus, you said that you'd help.'

Sitting down, Leighton pinched the bridge of nose and sighed. 'Look Vicki, regardless of your intentions, I don't think you can claim innocence on this one. I can't vouch for you.'

'Well, I had no other way of finding this.'

She turned the computer around, so Leighton could see the screen. The display featured a booking confirmation for a bus company called *Route King*. Details for a passenger called Miss L. Taylor had been entered, and a flashing line of text at the bottom of the screen stated, "transaction complete."

Leighton tugged a pair of horn-rimmed glasses from his jacket pocket, and peered at the computer.

'Leighton, these are the last pages Laurie accessed before she disappeared, so that proves she made a booking.'

'That's clearly evident, but, as I said,' Leighton sat back removing his glasses, 'Laurie may have never boarded the bus.'

'That's also true.' Vicki allowed this concession. 'But, the other thing that keeps me awake is the fact this bus company may not actually exist.'

'What do you mean?'

'They don't exist - not in yellow pages, not online, and not according to any of the bus depots I checked.'

'You checked?'

'I've searched; they don't exist anywhere on any record.'

'Look, this is madness,' Leighton sighed, as he raised a hand to request a cheque from a waitress. 'I think I'll head back to Oceanside. We're done here.'

'Madness?' Vicki's eyes widened in frustration. 'How can you not see this?'

'Listen, so far, what we have is a girl whose friend didn't show up to meet her. How many times do you think that happens every day?' Leighton checked himself for raising his voice and dropped his volume. 'Then, that same friend feels embarrassed, and decides rather than deal with the fallout, they'll just slip off the radar for a few weeks.'

As Vicki stared at the floor in defeated silence, a waitress lifted the plates and a couple of twenties from the table.

'Come on,' Leighton said, as he stood up. 'I'll drop you home.'

He walked to the door. Vicki, however, remained deliberately seated, as if bolted there.

'No, you go ahead, I'll take a bus.' She flashed a bitter smile. 'Should be safe enough on public transport out here, right?'

'Look, don't be childish,' he called back to her from the doorway, 'You just-'

'Childish!' Vicki's eyes narrowed. 'You want to see childish, Detective, how about this?'

Vicki stood up, picked up the computer, and walked past Leighton. She stepped out of the diner into the hot sun, where, lifting the laptop above her head, she threw it forward, smashing it into plastic fragments on the pavement.

'What the hell are you doing?' He tried to take Vicki by the arm, but she shook him off.

'She's not simply gone off somewhere; something bad has happened, Leighton,' she said, her eyes already glazed with suppressed tears. 'Why the hell can't you see that?'

'I'm done here,' Leighton said calmly, stepped off the sidewalk, and crossed the street to his car. 'I did what you asked, Miss Reiner,' he called without turning around.

'Hey,' Vicki shouted to his back. 'You were done with this case before you even started,' she added angrily. 'God, if this is your attitude, Leighton, the force is better off with you being retired.'

Dismissing her with a wave of his hand, he opened his car and climbed in.

He spun the car noisily around, and pulled up next to her. Rolling down the window, he leaned towards her. 'Are you getting in?'

'Go to hell!' Vicki said, as she crouched on the ground and began sifting through the pieces of plastic and smashed circuits from the pavement.

Leighton looked at her for a moment - just long enough to ensure she had her purse over her shoulder - then, without another word, he drove off.

14

At 10:15 a.m. Monday morning, Bradley McGhee was one pissed-off man. That swaggering pain in the ass Anthony Morrelli should have shown up for work over three hours ago, only he hadn't appeared. The tourists had bought their tickets in advance from the hotel reception, two dozen of them had arrived at the marina - cameras at the ready, and eager to get out on the water. Only there was no Anthony waiting there to greet them. The crowd, who were already pissed off at getting their designer slacks damp from the river water, grew restless.

Between him and Sandy - the boat pilot - the two of them had somehow got all the clients strapped in and seated, but the entire process had taken a good forty minutes longer than it should have.

Damn it, Anthony Morrelli could never have won any prizes for sincerity, but he knew how to fill up a boat with out-of-towners in under ten minutes - and that was a skill Bradley valued. Therefore, he would not follow his instinct and tell Anthony to stick a flare gun up his ass and pull the trigger; instead, he would simply remind him the working week had started and his presence at the marina was respectfully requested.

Once the clucking tourists were out on the river, Bradley walked back along the marina to the long white trailer that served as an office. Sitting down in his massage chair, he picked up the grubby telephone, and called Scotty's Bar to see if his only boatman was enjoying an unplanned Monday of playing skittles with beer bottles. While it rang, Bradley scratched at his crotch with his free hand.

A female voice answered, 'Hello, Scotty's,' she said brightly.

'Who is this?'

'Marianne, why?'

'Honey, this is Bradley McGhee of BBM River Tours…'

'Drop off some fliers, I'll put them out front.'

'Whoa, hang on. Kind as that offer is, I'm actually looking for one of your regulars.'

'Oh, who?'

'Anthony Morrelli. Is he up there today?'

'He owe you some money?'

'No, nothing like that. He works for me down here on the water, but he didn't show up this morning.'

'Anthony was in Friday night, had a skin-full, as I recall, and stayed till closing time, but that was the last time I saw him.'

'Okay.' Bradley sighed. 'You sure?'

'Hang on. Let me just check with Maria. She was on last night.'

There was a dull clatter as the phone was laid down, then Bradley could hear the clinking of glasses being stacked and the distant strains of "La Bamba." After a few moments, the phone was picked back up.

'Hello?'

'Hey.'

'Okay, I couldn't find Maria - probably out back having a smoke - but I checked with Janine; she was on last night, too. She said Anthony wasn't in at all yesterday, or last night. You tried his house?'

'Yeah,' Bradley lied. 'Thanks for your help.'

'Okay, I'm sure he'll turn up.'

'Listen, honey, if he does show up, and if he's been on the sauce – can you please dump him into a cab, and send him back down this way?'

'Sure thing.'

Bradley hung up the phone and dragged a hand over his weathered face. In six years, Anthony had never taken so much as a sick day. Something was wrong here, but in his mind, Bradley assumed Anthony Morrelli had found a new job, or a woman with a hot body, or something good enough to keep him away.

He reached into a drawer in his cheap desk, and pulled out a sheet of A4 paper and a Sharpie pen. He yanked the cap off, the pen releasing a vinegar vapour. Then, he wrote out four words in block letters: HELP WANTED ENQUIRE WITHIN.

15

As he negotiated a worn cassette tape into the player, Leighton sighed. Vicki's bloody-minded fixation on her friend's unlikely demise bordered on obsessive. As the twang of "Delta Blues" filled the car, Leighton set his eyes on the road ahead, and tried to let the miles drift by. However, the emotional fallout from his departure was still bouncing around in his restless mind - drawing him back to his past like a bungee cord.

Leighton would have questioned why he had ever agreed to go along to Barstow in the first place, but he knew the answer to that. Nothing about the missing girl in any way interested him, but Vicki herself was quietly fascinating. Five decades earlier, when Leighton had been a child attending junior school, his teacher was a dark-haired, softly spoken woman, who smelled of lavender. On some occasions, she would come to sit by Leighton, and show him how to sketch, or read. In these moments, the small boy would feel a strange, tingling sensation, as if an aura of energy emanated from the woman. He would feel his skin fizz in response to her soft voice, as she drew shapes for him to follow, or guided his eyes along unfamiliar words. Now, all these years later, something about Vicki recreated that strange feeling - a simple sense of connection with another human being. It felt strangely right.

Despite this, she was still an absolute pain in the ass.

That fact did little to ease Leighton's guilt at abandoning a girl in her twenties to make her own way home, especially up here along Route 15. An image of a stormy night filled his mind. The recollection was so real, he could feel the warm, thrumming rain battering down like bullets.

Leighton breathed out and gently pushed the thought away until later. That was what his grief counsellor had taught him to do. Trying to suddenly block out the thought didn't work; he had to blow it away softly, otherwise it would bounce right back into his mind.

An impatient truck horn blasted him back into the moment. Leighton slowed down, and allowed the heavy, rumbling vehicle to pass him.

'Okay,' he said to the air, thinking he could come up with a way to help Vicki.

Leighton decided to approach it from a new angle. He would assume Vicki was somehow correct in her suspicions, and consider what he would do, if that was the case. It was, of course, a simply academic exercise. The girl was clearly blowing things out of proportion, but fully investigating her flawed beliefs would throw up a set of facts she would not be able to ignore. That way, at least he wouldn't just be asking Vicki to ignore a situation. Instead, he'd provide her with evidence of an entirely different, and less dramatic, situation altogether, which would hopefully be more realistic.

Leighton needed to consider the starting point of the investigation. As he cruised along the highway, he decided he would speak to the ladies down at Oceanside dispatch. If this bus had shown up in the terminal, like Vicki had claimed, they should be able to track its journey. A pre-booked bus would also have a passenger record, which meant they would discover if Laurie was even on the bus - something that seemed increasingly unlikely.

That was fine. Leighton smiled, and began to drum along on the steering wheel in time to the music. He felt confident he was on the verge of giving Vicki her life back.

As the car curved along the smooth road, it moved out of the warm sunshine and into the relative shade of the National Park. The fragrance of desert lavender wafted through the air conditioner. Within a kilometre or so of entering the park, Leighton noticed a Highway Patrol motorcycle parked in a lay-by on the opposite side of the road.

He glanced for a moment at the bike parked at the side of the road, and slowed long enough to confirm there was no visible officer or other vehicle nearby. For a second, Leighton considered turning around to check out the situation, but then, he shook the thought away. The biker would be talking a leak, or having a smoke. In either case, he wouldn't appreciate the intrusion of some paranoid ex-detective stalking him through the trees.

He smiled a crooked smile, and thought to himself seeing danger on every highway was simply a sign he had spent too much time with Vicki.

16

It was one of those fresh early mornings, where a bright haze gave the air a cool quality with the promise of certain heat to come. The moisture, which was still rising like a phantom from the sandy earth, would probably burn off by noon, leaving a clear blue sky over Nevada.

At 5:45 a.m., Jennifer Sanchez stood on a dry footpath in the Mojave National Park, and peered intently in all directions. The area surrounding her was full of silent cacti, and, moments earlier, her dog had vanished amongst them. She wasn't sure of the exact moment he had vanished, because once off the lead, Rasputin would race off in crazy loops - darting ahead, then swooping into the boulders and shrubs, only to appear moments later behind her. She had thrown a couple of arid sticks for him, which he had obediently retrieved, but Jen could tell he was more interested in burning off some energy speeding around beneath the trees. So, she had let him go. It had been a bad move. The excited dog thundered into the tangle of bushes five minutes earlier, but then failed to reappear again.

Sighing in frustration, Jen felt a sudden dip in early morning temperature, and zipped up her red Nike top. Stamping her feet impatiently, she peered around, but found no sign of her dog.

'Ra!' she called loudly. The eruption of sound startled a cloud of birds from a nearby bush.

Still nothing.

The walk through the park was a journey Jen would make every morning. Usually, she would feely utterly safe as she wandered the dusty, desolate paths, which sliced through the rocky landscape National Park. This was because she was accompanied by Rasputin - a fourteen-year-old, German shepherd.

Each morning, she would leave her Jeep in the westerly parking lot, which was really nothing more than a large clearing hemmed in by rough wooden fences. There were rarely any other vehicles there, other than the odd people-carrier with a bike rack, or the previous day, when a random old bus had appeared in one shadowy corner of the clearing.

At that end of the car park, almost touching the fence, was a small roofed shelter. One side of this structure featured a laminated map of the various walking routes fastened with brass tacks to the wooden wall; the opposite wall was lined with a rack of fire brushes - the old broom style - made by tied twigs. This feature always freaked the child within Jen out a little. Even now, at the age of forty-three, she clearly remembered seeing them as young girl when her parents had taken the family for fresh air and summer picnics. She recalled stepping out of her father's stifling car into the bustling excitement of the National Park, where she would creep up on whirring crickets, and chase butterflies in the dappled light. When she had asked her older sister what the shelters were, she had told Jen in a conspiratorial whisper the ragged structures were where desert witches would park their broomsticks, before creeping amongst the boulders to gather snakes and lizards, or, if they were lucky, lost children.

After that, Jen would only go into the park if she held her mother's hand, and picnics became more about scanning the shadows beneath the trees than enjoying the food. Thankfully, the fear of dark witches dissolved as she grew older, and it was not until Jen bought the retired police dog from the shelter and began frequenting the park again that she even thought about it.

As an adult, Jen had rediscovered the pleasure of the wild outdoors as part of her recovery. After spending ten years in a miserable marriage, in a claustrophobic little house, she had somehow found the strength to get divorced, and take back her life. The anti-depressants she had swallowed nightly during her marriage were poured down the sink and replaced with early morning walks, carrot juice, and fifteen minutes of nightly meditation. Whether it was being rid of her sulky husband, or simply her new routine, Jen had felt less anxious and much happier than she had in months, possibly even years.

Usually, she loved starting her day with fresh air and a bit of easy exercise. However, today, the woods felt different somehow. Perhaps it was simply quieter than usual.

'Ra, come on boy!' she called again.

There was an excited bark from somewhere nearby. Jen turned around to see the big dog leaping through the long needle grass, like a dolphin breaking through a yellow sea.

'Come on, you silly old mutt,' Jen laughed.

At a point about ten metres along the path, Rasputin burst out of the undergrowth. Jen felt her shoulders slump with relief. The dog looked towards her, and began to excitedly wag his tail from side-to-side. Still, he did not move towards her, so Jen called again.

'Come on, Ra, come on,' she called, and patted her leg.

In response to this, the big dog came running excitedly along the path towards her. As he grew nearer, something bizarre caught Jen's eye. At first glance, she thought the limp grey object dangling from Rasputin's mouth was a glove or perhaps a Halloween prop, but then, he reached her, and dropped the object at her feet.

The bitter sweet stink of decay from the mottled hand caused Jen to instinctively turn away and retch. She waved a flapping hand back towards the dog, who promptly picked up the hand again, then dropped it even closer to her. Jen moaned again, and forced her eyes away from it. Rasputin, who believed his mistress was pleased, barked excitedly, and rushed back into the undergrowth to retrieve the rest of the body parts.

17

Vicki exited the cab, and slung her bag over her shoulder. The last couple of days had taken its toll on her, but she wasn't ready to give up just yet. If anything, the trip to Barstow had given her a new resolve to uncover the truth. However cathartic it had been, her tantrum outside the diner had been the quickest way she could retrieve the SATA hard drive from the laptop. As she had cleaned up the debris from the street, she had slipped the thin metal case into her bag. If she had in any way believed Laurie was safe and well, Vicki would not have been so destructive with her property. As it was, she had little doubt of the tragic nature of her friend's absence.

The initial shock and pain of Laurie going missing had strangely been put on pause, replaced by frustration and a burning commitment to find out the truth. Leighton's dismissive attitude was only a blip. Vicki knew she had the technical expertise to investigate what happened herself. Now she had the hard drive, she would be able to locate the precise cluster and host of the bus website. More importantly, she could run a bloodhound programme to tear through any encryption, and discover the name of the web author who maintained the site.

As she struggled to turn her key in the lock, she could hear the telephone ringing from the other side of the door. Fumbling, she opened the door, stepped inside, and closed it with her foot. She then punched a four-digit code into a small touchpad panel in the hallway.

By the time she had deactivated the alarm, the phone had fallen silent.

Vicki wandered down the hallway, into her bedroom where she dumped her bag on her bed. Slumping down on the mattress next to it, she reached across to where her laptop sat on the nightstand.

She opened up the device and it hummed and clicked to life.

Swiping her fingers across the glowing screen, she opened an electronic folder entitled 'Laurie'. This was the location in which she had saved copies of the all the information she had gathered. Taking Laurie's computer drive from her bag, she placed it next to her own laptop and then knelt on the floor beside the bed. She reached into the dark space beneath the bed and pulled out a plastic box of computer cables and connectors. For a moment, she rummaged through the nest of cables before finally pulling on the one she required. As the black cable slid free from the others, the phone in the hallway began ringing again. Vicki sighed and levered herself up from the bedroom floor. The phone continued to ring insistently, until Vicki stumbled towards it, and picked up the handset.

'Hello?' she panted.

'Victoria. It's your mother.'

'Hi, sorry, I was just along in the bedroom.'

'Are you sitting down yet?'

'Why?' Vicki felt a sudden rush of adrenaline flood her body.

'I have some rather unpleasant news for you.'

'What is it?'

'Your father's dead,' her mother said.

Vicki felt the ground soften then melt beneath her feet. 'What did you say?' she asked quietly.

'He was found this morning.'

'What happened?' Vicki was speaking, but she was not thinking about anything; all her thoughts had simply stopped.

'Apparently, he had taken to gathering herbs from around the cabin, and infusing his own tea. We won't know for certain until the toxicology report is completed, but it looks like he included belladonna amongst his mint and nettles.'

'He's dead?'

'Yes, honey, he's dead. I'm sorry.'

Vicki's mother continued speaking, twittering on indifferently about the lack of funeral plans, but her daughter had slipped silently on to the floor. She let the telephone fall from her hand. Her mind was consumed by a distant memory from the first summer they had moved to Oceanside. Back then, her mother was already perpetually lost to her career. Her father, who perhaps in some cosmic way sensed his limited time, was more content to collect his daughter from kindergarten, and spend afternoons on the beach digging for treasure with plastic spades and wooden spoons. Now, two decades later, Vicki sat - half a kilometre from the spot where she and her father had gathered shells and followed in each other's footsteps spiralling around the sand - and wept.

Her father was lost to eternity.

18

On the afternoon Leighton had returned from Barstow, he stopped in at the police station. The place was busy following a botched robbery of a jeweller's shop, so Leighton had left a message for dispatch with Lenny at reception. He heard nothing back for two days, and consequently assumed he was now of little significance to the people in the station.

Leighton had been frying off some chopped garlic, with cubes of pancetta, to make a pasta sauce, listening to a hissing Rolling Stones vinyl album on his stereo, when he heard the dull buzz of the doorbell, one evening. He turned off the gas, turned down the music, and walked through the apartment to the front door.

Wiping his hands on a tea towel, he partly hoped to find Vicki standing there, but it wasn't.

'Hi, Jonesy,'

'Wendy.' Leighton smiled warmly. 'In you come. Now, if the boss has sent you to woo me back to work …'

The dispatch officer laughed heartily at the idea as she entered the house. As she moved by him, Leighton noticed she was clutching a manila envelope.

'I think if the boss knew I was here passing on information, we'd both be spending the night in the cells.'

'Too true. Now, you grab a seat, and I'll fix you a drink.'

'It's okay, Jonesy,' Wendy said, as she sat on the coffee-coloured sofa, 'I've got two teenagers in the car, who are itching to get to Taco Bell for supper.'

'Sounds good.' Leighton smiled to conceal his lie.

'Judging by the yummy smell in here, you'll be eating better than us.'

'I'm not sure. My creations can often go either way.'

Leighton sat opposite the woman, who bore the troubled expression of someone carrying bad news to pass on. It was an expression he knew well.

'Listen, Jonesy. That note you left the other day about checking out that bus …'

'Yeah?'

'Well, the Chief picked it up at reception, and went crazy. He told Lenny after your retirement you were now a member of the public, and you can't make demands on police time. He even ripped up your note, and tossed it in the trash behind reception.'

Leighton rolled his eyes. 'Guess I should have shown up for his goddamn party.'

Wendy smiled. 'You know him too well.'

'Hey, it's fine.' Leighton shrugged. 'I didn't want anyone getting into bother on account of me. I'll get on to checking out the bus myself.'

Wendy shook her head. 'Don't worry - we backroom rebels in dispatch don't pay too much attention to the Chief. I just want you to be careful. You can't just show up the station, without the Chief trying to run you out of town.'

'Thanks, Wendy.'

'Anyway, the thing is, Lenny fished out the note and brought it to me, and I did a bit of digging - off the record.'

'And?'

'I mean it, Jonesy, you're a charming old bastard, but this never came from me.'

'You have my word,' Leighton said, and held a hand to his heart.

'This gets out, and you'll have my family to feed, and they take some feeding.'

Wendy leaned across and handed Leighton the manila envelope.

'What's this?'

'I spoke to Kevin Harris over at the Traffic Control Centre - our kids used to play in little league together, and I'd often pick up his two, along with my own brats, so he owes me a favour or two.'

'Don't we all?' Leighton said.

'I gave him the details and locations, and he emailed me the camera views from the bus depot and the major roads through the city.'

Leighton opened the envelope, withdrawing a bundle of black and white prints of areas of the city. Each image featured details of time and location in neat white letters on the bottom right corner.

'They're in order,' Wendy continued. 'If you look at the first one, taken at Escondido, you can see the bus entering the depot. The next photograph shows it leaving the depot, sixty-six seconds later.'

Leighton nodded, and then, flicked through several more pictures. 'I don't see it in any of the other prints.'

'Exactly!' Wendy leaned forward. 'Your bus left that depot, but didn't show up on any of the major routes. I don't know where the hell it went after that, but it certainly didn't come through Oceanside after leaving the terminal.'

'You sure?' Leighton frowned.

'The camera doesn't lie, Jonesy. That bus just vanished.'

'How weird?'

'Yeah, talking of weird, I have two ravenous teenagers in a car, who will be drooling on my leather trim by now.'

As she stood up, Wendy glanced around. 'Hey the place looks nice, Jonesy. You expecting company and tidied up?'

'No,' Leighton chuckled. 'I like tidy.'

'Yeah?' Wendy sighed. 'You must be the only man on the West Coast who does.'

Leighton walked her to the door and as she turned to leave his doorstep, he took Wendy's hand.

'Thank you for doing this.'

Wendy brushed her other hand dismissively in the air.

'I mean it,' Leighton said softly. 'I never made many friends at the precinct, but you've always been good to me.'

'Ah, you're better than you think, Jonesy. Just take care of yourself.' She gave him a quick kiss on the cheek, and hurried to the car. Halfway there, she turned around, just as Leighton was about to close his door.

'Hey,' she called, 'I almost forgot, something.'

'What - to ask for gas money?'

'It's probably nothing, but an internal bulletin came through this evening from Highway Patrol. Apparently one of their bikers failed to return to the station at the end of his shift. They're asking all emergency services to be vigilant. Whatever that means.'

'Thanks, I'm always vigilant,' Leighton said.

'I think you mean virginal,' Wendy said with a laugh and then hurried into her car.

After Wendy had left, Leighton did not return to the stove to complete preparing the rest of his dinner. Instead, he went to the refrigerator poured a tall glass of rum and ice, and returned to his sofa. He then spent almost an hour looking through the twelve grainy photographs. Leaving his drink untouched, he eventually went to a kitchen drawer and returned with a phonebook. He sat beside the scattered photographs as he flicked through the white pages, before and he eventually stopped at the Asian Restaurant section.

19

There were three initial stages to Charlie Thomson's terror. The first was his physical situation. He awoke to find himself weak-limbed, and lying on his back in a dark structure. A throbbing pain deep in his head seemed strong enough to temporarily obliterate any memory of how he had arrived at this location. The fact he had been wrapped in plastic sheeting, like a slaughtered pig, and placed in the bowels of the rumbling bus as it travelled miles into the hills was, perhaps fortunately, unknown to him.

Despite his mind still being shrouded in the remnants of the tranquilliser, he was vaguely aware the building was large and dark, stretching perhaps twenty feet in all directions around him. As his eyes grew accustomed to the darkness, Charlie twisted his head from side to side, trying to locate some point of reference. He could distinguish large grey squares attached to the distant walls. Each of these squares seemed to feature a regular pattern of dark spots. Something about this pattern seemed familiar to Charlie, and he had to search through the fog of his mind to find the association.

The terror rose within him when he realised that the walls were lined with sheets of egg cartons. Eleven years earlier, Charlie had played bass guitar in a couple of bands in his senior year at Oceanside High School. On Tuesday afternoons, he and the other guys would rock out in a small practice room lined with the same type of egg cartons. It seemed so remarkable to him at the time that, outside of the room, no sound could be heard, even when the guitars were screaming out within.

The realisation that the walls of his prison had been sound-proofed triggered Charlie's second wave of terror. He had to get out of this place, regardless of how numb his limbs felt, but as he attempted to move his legs and arms, he found himself unable to. For a moment, he wondered if he was actually paralysed – however, his hands moved freely below the wrist. Charlie shifted his trembling head enough to see his hands were attached, by orange cable ties, to the table, which felt hard and cold beneath his sweating skin.

It was then he began to comprehend he was not lying on some makeshift surface; it was a stainless-steel table, like those found in surgeries or industrial kitchens.

Charlie's final stage of terror came when, he twisted around far enough to see what was located over each of his shoulders. There were two black tripods. One featured a large black video camera, on which a small red LED light was blinking; the other held a massive light bulb surrounded by the type of white umbrella used by photographers. As he realised the horror of his situation, Charlie began to thrash crazily against his unforgiving restraints until his face was scarlet, dripping with sweat, and his heart was hammering against his rib cage. If he hoped to have any chance of escape, he would have to calm down and try to think clearly.

Taking a deep breath, he closed his eyes and expelled the air as slowly as he could. This started to have a calming effect, so he repeated the breathing exercise, focussing purely on inhaling and exhaling. After several moments, he felt his heart return to an almost regular pace. As he calmed down and opened his eyes, Charlie was overcome by the feeling that he was being watched.

'Ah good, you're awake,' said an excited voice from the darkness. 'Now, we can get started...'

20

The evening sun was setting as Leighton pulled his car off the road, and parked on the communal lot of the Oceanside housing complex. The location was essentially a two-storey condominium of eight beach side homes.

As he wrenched on the parking brake, Leighton glanced around. His car looked conspicuously grubby, as it sat uncomfortably amongst the porches and BMWs. This made Leighton smile proudly. He pulled a scrap of paper from his pocket and checked the address. When he had picked up Vicki the previous week, he collected her from the car park, and so he avoided having to approach the formidable white block of homes. This time was different. Having checked the property number, he stuffed the paper back in his jacket, walked to the trunk of his car, opened it, and took out two white paper bags.

Leighton traversed the path to the apartment, and pressed the doorbell, shifting from foot to foot as he nervously waited.

After a few minutes, the door opened.

'Hi,' Vicki said looking slightly confused.

Leighton thought she looked tired, and maybe something else, too.

'Hey,' he greeted her. 'I'm sorry for just showing up like this. I wanted to apologise. I tried calling for a couple of days…'

'It's not a great time, Detective. I get why you're here.' She rubbed her temples. "I get it - I was stupid okay?"

Leighton's expression became uncharacteristically soft. 'Hey, it's fine,' he said, 'I just wanted see you – to say I'm sorry about Monday.'

Vicki looked at him for a moment, then sighed.

'It's okay, come on in.'

She walked ahead, leaving Leighton to close the large door behind him.

Vicki didn't turn around as she led him along a small hallway to a large open plan room with patio doors opening to a beach front balcony. Leighton's eyes widened at the impressive view of the orange sky above the pounding ocean.

'Have a seat.' Vicki waved a hand towards the two red sofas.

'I brought you this.' Leighton held up one of the bags.

'What is it?' Vicki frowned inquisitively.

'That stuff you said you liked from Thai Garden – fried Tofu and spring rolls. Is that right?'

'Wow.' Vicki's eyes widened. 'That was really thoughtful of you…'

This simple act was too much for Vicki, who was unable to hold back the tears that began forming beneath her eyes.

'My father died,' she said quietly. Her shoulders slumped, and the tears began pouring over her face.

'Oh, no, I'm sorry.' Leighton dropped the bags, moved over to Vicki, and held her. 'I'll go.'

For a few moments, she stayed there, sobbing against the comforting man, letting her hot tears wet his shirt.

'I'll go,' he said softly again as her heaving slowed and began to subside.

'No,' she said, pushing back from him, and wiping at her face. 'It's okay. You're just the first person I've told.'

'Do you want to speak about it?'

Vicki wiped at her red eyes with her sleeve. 'I guess.'

'Where is your mother?'

'Still in the city – she has the US MaxFac Conference this week. She said she'll aim to stop by next Friday.'

'But, what about the funeral?'

'There won't be one.' Vicki shrugged, 'My father was a member of the Natural Burial Foundation. He paid nine hundred to bucks to get buried wrapped in banana leaves in an undisclosed location.'

'Are you serious?'

'Unfortunately, yes.'

'I don't suppose you'll feel much like this.' Leighton looked at the bags on the floor.

'Actually, I'm starving. Not eaten for a couple of days. I'll get us some plates.'

'Us?'

'Yeah, looks like you've brought enough for a small army there.'

Leighton blushed. 'They had a few types; I didn't know which one you'd prefer.'

Vicki smiled, though her face was still wet from crying.

'It's only the tub of sauce that's different. You could have got one box of fried tofu and a couple of extra sauces. How many boxes did you get?'

'Four.' Leighton looked shamefully at his feet.

'Then, you're definitely eating, too!'

Vicki went to through to a dimly lit kitchen area and returned with two glossy white plates. She knelt on the floor, and divided the crispy tofu and a portion of noodles between the two of them.

'I must confess, I've never tasted tofu before.'

'Don't worry, it's nothing bad.'

'What's it like?'

'Just try it.'

Vicki handed him a plate, and went back to the kitchen, returning with two chilled bottles of imported beer. Sitting cross-legged on the floor next to Leighton she watched as he took his first tentative bite.

He looked upwards as he chewed and despite his reservations, he found he liked it.

'Well?' Vicki asked.

'Pretty good. Kind of like calamari, only softer.'

'See, I knew you were a gentleman of taste.'

Leighton picked up his cool bottle and held it out to her. Toasting before sipping was a sacred ritual amongst all officers.

Station houses were full of urban legends of officers who fell in the line of duty after they had forgotten to toast in a bar the previous evening.

'Cheers,' Leighton said.

Vicki clicked her green bottle against Leighton's, and they both took a gulp.

They ate in comfortable silence, but when Leighton noticed Vicki beginning to stare into the distance, he recognised a look he had often seen in his bathroom mirror.

'You know you can tell me about him, if you want?'

Vicki look startled for a second, then smiled. 'How did you…'

'It's a retired cop slash grieving father thing.' Leighton focussed his attention on selection a piece of food, but was intently hoping Vicki would trust him.

'There's not much to tell.' She sighed. 'I still don't feel it yet. It's weird - because he's been kind of distant for most of my adult life. Maybe I had less to lose.'

'Loss is loss.'

'I guess. Though, it sounds like something my dad would learn on his hippy retreats.'

Leighton looked at Vicki for a moment. Now, it was his turn to do some trusting – something he found difficult.

'You know, I never saw much of my daughter Annie once she hit high school,' he chuckled wryly. 'It was as if one minute, were making ant farms in the backyard, the next, she was sneaking out her bedroom window at midnight. It felt like I was suddenly cut out; I wanted to be involved, to keep her safe, but I guess, for her, it was suffocating. After her mother and I separated, I found myself trying to be mom and dad … and failing at both.'

'But, you loved her.'

'Yes, I did - with all my heart, but …' Leighton looked at the floor.

'But?'

'I'm not sure that's what she would have thought.'

'Why?' Vicki asked, as she shuffled slightly closer.

Leighton smiled and shrugged. 'That last year, our conversations were almost always just arguments. Did I love her? Yes. Was I proud of my baby girl? Hell, yes.' Leighton's voice cracked. 'But, I didn't know how to shoehorn these things into everyday conversation. It's not easy, to set boundaries and show love, and hold down a job and muddle through life at the same time.'

'I know, but some manage it.' Vicki said defiantly.

'That's true, but some people win the state lottery. Doesn't mean we all can. Look, I just mean, you maybe shouldn't judge your father by what he didn't say.'

'So, you think *my* father loved *me*?' As Vicki spoke, she met Leighton's gaze.

'Yes, I'm sure he loved you, very much.'

'Maybe, but he never said so. I mean, he called me "sweetheart," but never anything sincere.'

'That might be true.' Leighton conceded. 'But, did you always tell your father how you felt?'

Vicki reluctantly shook her head, and chewed on her bottom lip.

'We don't always say what we feel. That's the messed-up thing about humans.'

There was a moment of silence, in which they both felt the rich comfort of each other's presence.

'No, I guess not. So, you want a fresh beer?' Vicki held up her empty bottle.

'I'm good here, thanks.' Leighton smiled, and patted his stomach.

'Mind if I do?'

'Not at all.'

Vicki leapt up, leaving Leighton dipping some more fried food into a circular tub of chilli sauce. When she returned, she held two more beers. Ignoring Leighton's protests, she handed him one, and flopped on to a cushion on the floor beside him.

'So, you came over here to apologise, eh?'

'Yeah, I over-reacted. I'm sorry. I shouldn't have left you.'

'Thanks. Consider yourself forgiven. Tofu works every time.'

'Listen, Vicki, I also found out some stuff that paints a different light on the case.'

'What, about Laurie?'

'I can fill you in later. You have enough to deal with now.'

'Leighton,' Vicki said firmly, 'God knows I need a distraction now more than ever.'

He looked at her for a long moment. 'Well, I asked a friend to get me the CCTV camera footage of the bus you saw arrive at the depot. Did you see the front of the bus that afternoon?'

'Yeah, I mean, I think so.'

'Can you remember what it said?'

'Not really,' Vicki said, as she rubbed her temple again. 'San Diego, San Francisco, maybe.'

Leighton picked up the envelope from the floor beside him, took out a photograph, and handed to Vicki. 'Was this the bus you saw?'

Vicki peered at the black and white image for a moment, and nodded.

'Well, the thing is that this bus has "San Diego" displayed on the front, but it never went there, or to any of the places en route there.'

'How do you know that?'

'Traffic Control cameras cover the entire city. My friend obtained images from thirty-two cameras covering the routes north and south for the hour following the departure of that bus from the depot. Only those cameras covering the bus depot captured that bus.'

'So, maybe, it's still here, in the city?'

'Maybe, but I believe your bus showed up at Oceanside, then turned right around again.'

'But, why would it do that?'

'Well, the section of road up to Vegas isn't covered by any cameras.'

'No, I mean, why would it do that?'

'If something bad had happened…'

'Like what?' Vicki locked her unblinking eyes on to Leighton's. 'I want you to say it.'

Leighton looked to the open patio window, where the rhythmic waves continued their infinite motion. When he looked back, he found Vicki's eyes still fixed on his, demanding honesty.

'Like something bad happening on the bus,' he said quietly.

'What might that bad thing be?' Vicki pushed again.

'I don't know,' Leighton said.

'But it could be some type of crime, possibly?'

'Yes.' He eventually nodded. 'It is looking like a possibility. And, yes I am sorry that I was so dismissive.'

'Thank you.'

Leighton cleared the plates, cartons, and empty bottles to the kitchen area. Vicki brought her laptop and a pad of lined paper to the low coffee table. She sat on the floor and booted up the system.

'Okay, where do we start?' she said in a voice that sounded tinged with tiredness.

Leighton returned from the kitchen and sat beside her.

'I'm not sure. What do you think?' Leighton frowned, as he locked his fingers together beneath his chin.

'You're the cop!'

'I used to be,' he corrected.

'Okay, retired cop, whatever. Where would you start, if this was your "official case," given what you know already?'

Leighton looked intently at the photographs. They were stacked in a neat pile, with the uppermost image being that of the front of the bus. Given the quality of the image, it was impossible to make out the licence plate, which, in any case, would probably be false.

'We need to connect the bus to a person or persons. What about the web page you called up, advertising the service? Would a commercial company create that – someone on record?'

'Not likely, it was just a page. However, I might be able to trace who the domain is registered to.'

'The what?'

'You know, how every website has an address - the "www" bit?'

Leighton rolled his eyes. 'I'm not that far behind the times.'

'Good,' Vicki said, as she began typing into her laptop. 'In order to use that address a site creator has to register his or her site. If I can reveal how the site was created, I might be able to find a name.'

'Okay, what should I do, while you're working your technological voodoo?'

'You could make us some coffee. I already had a couple of beers before you arrived. I couldn't sleep at all last night – I figured they might help, but I'm feeling a bit droopy now.'

'At least your plan's working,' Leighton smiled, 'you do look pretty tired.'

'I can't rest now, maybe once the software is running.'

Leighton nodded, then quietly did as he was told. He knew there was an expanding virtual universe which one day would engulf him, but, for the moment, he intended to stay away from that place as long as possible. Despite his urge to take a lead role in the hunt for Laurie Taylor, he was content to take a step back, and allow Vicki to perform her alchemy – turning digital bytes into information he could use in the real world.

He returned, cups in hand, to find Vicki had used a short cable to connect a small flat metal box to her computer.

'What's that do?' he asked as he sat beside her.

'It's the memory from Laurie's laptop. The original website has been taken down, but I can access a snapshot of it still held in the temporary files.'

'Like our memories?'

'Yeah, pretty much. Only this one doesn't fade with time.'

For a moment, Leighton and Vicki glanced at each other and felt the shared connection of unspoken loss.

Vicki then looked back at the laptop, clicked on a couple of buttons, and launched a program called "Sniffer." Within a few seconds, rows of numbers began racing across the screen. Moments later, a list of web pages opened in a new window. Vicki ran her cursor down them, and clicked on the bottom one, causing the Route King checkout page to open.

'Okay,' she said. 'this is the bus company page, so let's see if we can link to it a person.'

She clicked on the window and the picture vanished, only to be replaced by rows of numbers and words.

'What's happened?' Leighton leaned suddenly forward. 'Have you lost it?'

'No.' Vicki smirked. 'It's meant to do that. I'm viewing it as code.'

'Ah.' Leighton pretended to understand.

Peering at the screen, Vicki began to tap furiously on the keyboard. She slowly shook her head. 'Damn! There's nothing here to indicate who authored the site. But, it does provide some data.'

'What about the "www" address part, does that help?'

'Not really, it's usually bogus.'

'That list you were looking at first, does that show the pages in the order Laurie viewed them?'

'Yeah, why?'

'Well, in previous cases where the situation was unclear, I would walk the path of the victim. Find out what they did on that final day. Retrace the route. Maybe we could take a virtual walk through?'

'Sure.'

Viewing the pages revealed Laurie had initially visited the website of her alma mater, possibly reliving her student days in a bout of nostalgia. The next set of pages related to weather and facilities in Oceanside. This made Vicki smile sadly. Finally, she had performed a Google search for buses, and located the Greyhound Coach homepage.

'I don't understand this,' Vicki said as she bit her bottom lip.

'What?'

'I don't see where the Route King's page came from. I mean she was on the Greyhound page for seven seconds, and then, out of nowhere, this window opened. She didn't go back to Google – it must have been an automatic pop-up.'

'So, could this page…' Leighton looked uncertainly to Vicki who nodded at him to continue. 'Could it have been activated or triggered by her search - is that even possible?'

'Sure.' Vicki yawned. 'Excuse me.'

'It's okay.' Leighton grinned. 'I have that effect on most people.'

'Don't be silly; I'm just tired. Anyway, most searches are recorded somewhere, and are used to predict future results, so I guess you could program a page to load in response to that. Hang on, there's something weird here …' Vicki clicked between windows.

'What is it?'

'It looks like the Greyhound site window opened twice simultaneously.'

'Maybe she clicked on it twice?' Leighton queried hopefully.

'Yeah - maybe. But, it's more likely that one of the pages was false - a dummy page designed to sit on top of the real one.'

'Like a mask?'

'Exactly. Like a mask.'

'But, why?'

'False pages are often used to collect bank details or scam users into giving up cash or personal information. However, they can also be used to show artificially inflated prices so guiding customers away from them and on to less reliable sites.'

'Ah.' Leighton shifted in his seat. 'Vicki, can I use the bathroom.'

'Sure,' she said and yawned, 'sorry, it's at the end of the long hallway on the right. The light's on the left wall as you enter.'

The brightly lit corridor was lined with framed sepia photographs of old New York. The first two doors in the hallway were open, and Leighton glanced in as he passed them. Two clinical looking bedrooms featured matching beige and chocolate bedding. Both were lit by identical bedside lamps. In one of the rooms, the bed was covered in a mixture of photographs that looked to have been taken from an overturned shoe box sitting amongst them. Leighton imagined Vicki had been looking through her past, when his arrival interrupted her. He sighed guiltily, and continued on to pass a neat office, a messier bedroom, and then the bathroom.

When Leighton returned, Vicki was curled up like a child, asleep on the sofa. Obviously the combination of exhaustion, beer and emotional turmoil had finally eclipsed her desperation to remain vigilant. Some process was happening on her computer, as rows of numbers filled the screen, and a small bar along the bottom recorded some gradual progress. Tiptoeing around her, Leighton returned the coffee cups to the kitchen, then returned, and knelt in front of the sleeping girl.

'Vicki,' he said softly. There was no response, just the quiet rise and fall of her breathing.

He figured the white vest and grey sweatpants wouldn't be enough to keep her warm so, he found a linen closet and returned with a fleece blanket.

Tucking it around her shoulders, he had to check himself from brushing her hair away from her face, as he had done to a smaller sleeping girl decades earlier. He lifted up the stack of photographs and the writing pad, and moved to the dining table, where he sat down and began making some basic notes. The facts were increasingly clear to him now. There was a missing girl who had never contacted anyone or returned to her home and job in over a month, there was also a dubious website that seemed to disappear right around the same time the girl did, and finally there was a bus that seemed to show up and vanish at will. Scratching out possible scenarios on the page, Leighton found that all of them seemed based upon the alarming possibility that Vicki had been right.

Leighton had only managed a page or so when his own eyes began to close. He had planned to rest his head on his arms for a moment, but the combination food and beer and the company had left him equally drowsy, and within moments, he too, was lost to sleep.

When he opened his eyes again, six hours had passed, and a stranger was standing over him, pointing a 9 mm gun at his head.

21

As the bus approached her, Martha Coombs was nervous as hell. At the age of sixty-seven, she had never left the town of Blythe, but ever since her Nigel, her son, had moved down to San Diego six months earlier, she had been determined to visit him for a few days. Nigel, thankfully, had taken care of organising the whole thing for her. Going down to the city hadn't been her first choice. Once or twice, she had called him up, and suggested he might come up to visit the old house - she could make his favourite meatloaf, but he had explained he had been too busy with work for that. Martha had lived a long time, and she wasn't entirely convinced this was the only reason behind her son's reluctance to visit.

From the age of five, Nigel Coombs had been such a sensitive and fey young man, who she had secretly believed was most likely gay. While his classmates would play whooping war games in the playground, Nigel would collect pretty flowers from the perimeter of the school grounds, and bring them home crushed in his satchel. She had never raised the issue of his sexuality with him, mainly because he was so sensitive such a conversation would prove more difficult for him than it would for her. So, she had waited patiently all through his teenage years for her growing son to confide in her. Even in his early twenties, when he had started working as a hairdresser in Blythe's only salon, and would come home to share the day's dramas with his momma, he never mentioned romance of any sort. Then, in the last few years, he had taken to spending entire evenings on his computer. Sometimes, late at night, when he thought she was asleep, she would hear the murmurs of other voices and giggles from his bedroom, as he spoke to that tiny camera.

Still, she couldn't criticise him – especially after he had taken the time to buy her a bus ticket. And he had explained it wasn't just an ordinary one, either - this one was for a new bus company, with real nice facilities. He had sent her a paper ticket through the mail, and told her to put it in safely in her purse straight away.

As the bus rumbled to a stop, Martha checked for the sixth time that the ticket was still in her white leather purse - which it was - then, adjusted the back of her permed hair. When the noisy doors hissed open, Martha was both surprised and relieved to see the bus driver - who was not much younger than herself - was a friendly looking man with a neat little white moustache. However, when she stepped on to the stairs and into the gloom of the bus, she saw almost all of the other passengers were men in their twenties or thirties. She smiled at the driver and held out the ticket.

'Now,' she said, 'my son bought this for me so if it's not right, you can take it up with him.'

'Not a problem, ma'am,' replied the grinning driver, who took her ticket, without even looking at it. 'You just find yourself a seat, and once you're comfy, we'll get moving.'

22

The hands of the woman holding the automatic handgun did not tremble. *This*, thought Leighton, *is someone who had spent sufficient time at a gun club, time to be comfortable gripping that heavy lump of power.*

'Who the hell are you, and what are you doing in my house?' Abigail Reiner asked.

'It's okay, ma'am,' Leighton said sounding suddenly alert

'Yes, I know it is now; I've called the police,' she said, as if to confirm his defeat. The woman was dressed in a navy blue suit finished off with some expensive looking jewellery.

'Mrs. Reiner,' Leighton held up a hand, 'I'm a friend of your daughter.'

'Ha,' she snorted. 'Somehow, I doubt that.' Stepping to one side, she peered at the kitchen area and ed distastefully at the beer bottles and food cartons. She then returned her attention to Leighton.

'Mrs. Reiner, my name is Leighton Jones, I'm a retired police officer, I was here speaking to Vicki about the disappearance of her friend - Laurie Taylor.'

Something shifted in the woman's cold expression.

'Let me see some identification.'

Leighton reached slowly into his jacket pocket and produced a worn leather wallet, which he held out to her.

Abigail Reiner took the wallet, as if it were infected, peered inside for longer than was necessary, then finally lowered the weapon. Her expression did not soften.

'As an ex-police officer, you should know better than to ply a naïve young woman with alcohol. If I discover you've touched her, I'll have you charged with sexual assault. Stay the hell away from my home, and my daughter!'

'She came to me - asked for her my help,' Leighton said, as he slipped on his jacket.

'My daughter is psychologically vulnerable at the best of times but especially so right now.'

'I heard about your husband and -'

'Ex-husband,' Abigail corrected.

'In either case, I'm sorry.'

'Yes, clearly. Men like you disgust me. Now, please, leave my house.'

As he rose from the chair, Leighton tried momentarily to glance at Vicki who remained asleep on the sofa, but the woman folded her slender arms, and shifted her body to ensure she blocked his view.

'I'm sorry I gave you a fright, ma'am,' Leighton said sincerely and walked the door.

'You didn't,' Abigail called victoriously after him.

Leighton stepped out of the Reiner apartment into the bright morning sunlight and the steady sound of the waves against the shore. All around him was an explosion of colour and fragrance from the pink and orange flowers fringing the white apartment.

As he walked to his car, Leighton reflected upon Vicki's relationship with her mother. It couldn't have been easy for her growing up beneath the crushing weight of such a formidable personality.

Driving out of the parking area, he was passed by a rookie in a black and white cruiser - no doubt responding to the false alarm. Thankfully, he had escaped just in time.

Leighton drove home, where, after the therapeutic benefit of a long hot shower, he dressed in a pair of charcoal chinos and a white shirt and sat, barefoot, at the metal table on his tiled patio. Before him, was a breakfast of black tea and a toasted cinnamon bagel spread with apricot preserve. Lying next to this was the envelope containing the bus photographs. After taking a bite of food, Leighton slipped open the envelope, and removed a pencil and the sheet of notepaper he had scribbled on. He had drawn a number of squares around the sides of the page. Within these boxes, he had noted certain relevant details. He had also drawn joined lines connecting several of the facts to each other.

Website booking	*Victim boarded bus*
Phone unused	*Website dead*
Victim's home empty	*Home undisturbed*
No show for work	*No reports of incident on bus*
Bus missing	*Victim still on bus?*

Picking up the pencil, he tapped it on the table for a moment, then began writing. Beneath the list of facts, Leighton now wrote a list of words followed question marks:

Hostage?

Intentional entrapment?

Complicit passengers?

It was these final two words that concerned Leighton most. To break the tension, he sipped his tea, and tried to put the pieces together. It had been easy to accept that Laurie may have been abducted from a truck stop restroom by some psycho, but the question of the bus remained. *Why would it pretend to be bound for San Diego, but never travel beyond the Escondido Bus Terminal?* Even if there had been some problem at the terminal that meant the bus couldn't continue, the disgruntled passengers would all have disembarked at the depot. More importantly, if some assault had taken place on an interstate bus, it would have been witnessed and reported by somebody.

Draining the bitter remnants of his tea, Leighton watched the hypnotic sway of the morning lawn sprinklers, as they spurted to life. He decided there was now enough of a case to make the whole thing official. He breathed a sigh of relief at the prospect of handing this messy burden on to somebody else. The somebody in question, was his steel-jawed former boss, Chief Roger Gretsch.

23

Mark tried to convince himself he was not deluded, as he stepped off the droning plane into the bright air of San Diego's Lindbergh Field Airport. Shambling down the steel ramp to the bus that would transfer him to the grey terminal building, he shouldered his rucksack, and pulled down his sunglasses. The blurry heat-haze rising from the tarmac made the planes on the fringe of the black-top appear to be melting.

It was still possible, he told himself, he would arrive at the Black Cat Club, and simply find Jo with a guitar slung around her neck, singing to a mesmerized crowd. She would be shocked, and perhaps pissed off, Mark had the gall to show up. They would initially make small talk, but he would eventually ask her why she hadn't been in touch. However, beneath the pleasantries, would be the message she was happy without him. What made the situation so bizarre was Mark simultaneously hoped this was and was not the case. He didn't want the rejection, but at least that would mean that she was okay.

In recent weeks, he had heard nothing from Jo. After giving her a few days to settle in with room to breathe, Mark had sent her a simple text message asking if she was okay. It felt needy, but there was nothing romantic about it – just a simple check in. His cell phone showed that the message had been delivered but never read. After a couple of weeks, of pouring foamy beers and serving burgers, Mark had deleted the original message. He realised that if Jo didn't want him in her life he should respect that. But on the previous Friday, he had the night off and had spent it drinking in his own bar. That evening a young local guy with an acoustic guitar had been singing. When he played a couple of Joni Mitchell songs,

Mark had been overcome with drunken nostalgia and felt the urge to call Jo, just to tell her and simply here her voice again after five long weeks. Standing in the windy alleyway at the side of the bar, he dialled her number and took a deep breath. There was a click and Mark momentarily felt his heart flutter, then an automated voice told him that the cell phone he was calling was switched off.

At closing time, Mark had staggered home and flopped on his bed. Holding his phone unsteadily in his hand, he looked through all of Jo's social media accounts. Her final post on Twitter had been on the night she left. Moments into her bus journey, she had taken a photo of herself and shared it with the caption.

'Off to start the next part of my musical adventure...'

After that, there had been no further posts. Mark's sense of unease grew as he looked at her Facebook page, which had also showed no activity since the day she left. The following morning, with a throbbing head, he had arranged to fly down, to his mind and heart at rest.

Today Mark stepped on to the juddering shuttle bus and moved aside as the other passengers clambered aboard. There were no seats on the vehicle, which was designed purely to shuttle passengers and their hand luggage. At the opposite end of the bus, Mark could see a group of young women, who were clearly on holiday and bristling with excitement, as they peered out of the window looking for landmarks. They nudged each other, and took photographs to share with on social networks. Mark glanced at them, envious of their freedom and vitality. He wished Jo had taken a flight down, instead of the damned bus.

The cab journey from the airport sped by in a blur as Mark tried to breathe life into the possibility Jo was okay. Somehow, the more real Mark could imagine the scenario, the more realistic it seemed to be.

After stopping at seemingly endless sets of traffic lights, the cab came to a stop on University Avenue, where the driver pointed out the bar on the opposite side of the street. Mark handed the driver a bundle of ten dollar bills and climbed out. Slinging his bag over one shoulder, he crossed the busy street, and found himself in front of a classical old building, with a neon silhouette of a freaked-out cat above the name.

Inside, the bar was dark, and smelled of fresh Mexican food. Some fliers advertising live music were scattered around the tables. Mark approached the bar, and was greeted by a tall, young man, with a pierced eye-brow.

'Hey.' He smiled at Mark. 'What you after?'

'A bottle of Anchor, please.'

As the barman opened a cold beer and placed in front of him, Mark pulled a scrunched bill from his pocket, and handed it to the younger man.

'Good choice of beer, man.'

'Cheers,' Mark replied, and took a mouthful of the tangy cold liquid.

'You want any food?' the barman asked, as his hand reached for a menu.

'No, thanks.' Mark shook his head. 'I'm actually here looking for a girl.'

'Aren't we all?'

'No, I mean a girl who maybe sings here?'

Something shifted slightly in the younger man's face, as if some internal doors were being shut. 'We have a lot of acts come through here. You a private investigator?'

'No.' Mark smiled at the idea. 'I'm not a psycho stalker, either. I run a small music bar up in Laughlin. The girl left on a mini-tour to come down here, only no-one's heard from her in weeks. I just wanted to know she got here safely.'

'Shit, that's not cool.'

'Her name is Jo. Can I show you a picture?'

'Sure,' the barman said, suddenly more sympathetic.

Mark reached into his shirt pocket and produced a photo of Jo, standing outside the RPM shop, with her guitar in hand. It was one he had taken just after one of their first lunchtime picnics. At the time, he had pretended the photo would be a good promo shot for both the shop and the bar. In truth, he had simply wanted a photograph that beautiful, enchanting girl. Perhaps he naïvely thought it would help him hold on to her. Mark had the photo printed out at a local photo booth, with the vague intention of pinning it up behind the bar. Instead, he had considered it too precious to share, and kept it secretly in his wallet instead. He handed the photo to the barman, who peered at it for long moment.

'Sorry, man, never seen her.'

'Maybe she came in on your night off?'

'I'm full time here, five till eleven, seven days a week. There is no night off.'

'Is there only one Black Cat in San Diego?'

'Yeah.' The bar man nodded. 'Just the one, but there is another place up in San Fran. You could try there, but to be honest man, if I were you…'

'Yeah?'

'I reckon I'd call the cops. It could be serious, you know what I mean?'

'Yeah.' Mark nodded solemnly. 'I do.'

At that point, a group of perfumed young women clattered through the door of the Black Cat and absorbed the barman's attention. Mark picked up his beer, and relocated to a bright red leather chair by a table in a dark corner of the bar. After taking another drink from the bottle, he pulled the photograph out of his pocket again, and held it in both hands.

For a few moments, he stared at the image as if trying to open a window to the past he could somehow tumble through.

Eventually, he sighed, and reached into his back pocket. Taking out his phone, he slid his finger across the screen, and tapped in the internet search. When the number came up, he pressed it, and raised the phone to his ear. There were a couple of rings, then a voice answered.

'Good afternoon, Laughlin Police Department, how may I help?'

'I'd like to report a missing person,' Mark said, weakly hoping he was being stupid, but suspecting he wasn't.

24

Leighton had only taken two steps inside the cool vault of the station when he was met by Chief Gretsch, who had been supervising the installation of a new framed display of decorated officers on the wall behind the main reception. The Chief's own grinning photograph was at the top of the display. He hurried cross the foyer to intercept Leighton, before he reached the reception desk. As he blocked Leighton's path, he smiled a broad and emotionless smile.

'Mr. Jones, I was wondering when you might show up.' He took Leighton's arm, and led him purposefully across the marble floor, away from the reception desk.

'Excuse me?'

'Well, it seems you were in last week, too. You do know you are currently retired, right?' Gretsch chuckled without warmth.

'I just popped in.' Leighton shrugged. 'Didn't think there was any harm.'

'No?' A fresh smile split Gretsch's face. 'Well, that's as may be, *Mr. Jones*, but the way I see it is, you have attempted to misappropriate police resources, and trespassed on private property.'

'I was looking into a missing person for a young woman, who *asked* for my help.'

'This wouldn't be the same *young woman* whose mother called the station this morning to accuse you of stalking and harassment? And are you aware the *young woman* has a history of mental health issues?'

Leighton shook his head in disbelief.

'Now, you listen to me, Jones. I know a few cops who struggle with retirement, and start to convince themselves they see armed robberies taking place on every other street corner. It's an occupational hazard. My advice is you drop whatever Columbo case you're on right now, before you end up in front of a judge yourself. You're sixty years old, man. Go buy yourself a toy dog or a chess set.'

With his speech finished, Gretsch straightened his shirt, and walked away from Leighton, who decided to give the chief the benefit of the doubt.

'Sir,' he called loudly across the foyer. 'I believe we may have a group of highly organised killers working together.'

Gretsch turned around, as if he'd just been punched on the shoulder, and hurried back across the tiled floor to Leighton.

'A group?' As he spoke, the complexion of Gretsch's moisturised face darkened visibly.

'Well, more than two, anyway - there would probably have to be a driver and two others ...'

'Are you shitting me, Jones?'

'No, sir, I simply think that ...'

'No, you're clearly not thinking, are you, eh? Do you know what the collective noun for serial killers is?'

'No, sir, I don't believe I do,' Jones said, as he looked at his feet.

'Of course you don't, because there isn't one! They are loners by definition.'

'What about Bianchi and Buono, or Lake and Ng up in San Francisco? I bet their twenty-five victims might disagree with you, had they not been all been raped, tortured, and murdered.'

'Don't get fucking smart with me, Jones.' Gretsch said in an angry whisper. 'That was a pair, not a group. Anything more than that can't happen.'

'Or it hasn't, until now. Maybe before Lake and Ng, unimaginative cops blissfully believed serial killers working in pairs couldn't *happen* either.'

Gretsch stared directly at Leighton. 'Okay, let's cut the shit - to date, you have misappropriated police resources, trespassed on private property, and have been accused of harassment.' He pointed a stubby finger at Leighton. 'Given your monumental fuckup with that business at Black Mountain Ranch, I reckon you should keep your head down. So, if you show up here, or engage in communication with any of my officers, I'm throwing your ass in jail, Jones. Now, get the fuck out of here.'

This time, when Gretsch thundered off in a cloud of self-importance, Leighton let him go. The comment about the Ranch was a pretty low blow - even for Gretsch. However, it wasn't enough to deter Leighton; he was becoming used to rejection.

25

The gears of the bike clicked solidly into place, as Cherylyn Sanderson pedalled steadily along the smooth asphalt outside the dusty, desert city of Twenty-Nine Palms. After six weeks of early morning journeys, covering a grand total of ninety miles, her tanned legs were finally becoming more defined. Hitting the road at 6:30 a.m. each day wasn't easy, but it was a lot easier than it would be during the day, when the scorching sun was high in the sky and the thundering trucks began to dominate the hot roads.

At the age of thirty-seven, Cherylyn had decided it was time to fight nature's insistence on attaching extra inches to her body, and cycling was the easiest and least conspicuous way to do it. When anyone from work passed by in a car, she could pretend she was taking it easy - enjoying the view; however, once they had passed and she was alone again, she would push her body to a fat burning level. Cherylyn could have used the fitness facilities at work but that way, everyone would have known what she was up to.

Although she still found it difficult to believe, Cherylyn had worked on the reception of the busy Country Inn in the city of Twenty-Nine Palms for two decades. For most of that time, she had worked alongside Louisa - a small, round woman, fifteen years her senior. This meant for the majority of her adult life, Cherylyn had been defined by a favourable contrast to her co-worker. Whenever guests asked for her, they would refer to the young slim girl from reception. In the blissful bubble of youth, this was not something Cherylyn considered complimentary; it was simply factual. Nor did she give any consideration to how such comments must have made Louisa feel … until recently.

Six months earlier, Louisa had announced her retirement to spend more time helping her daughter with the grandchildren over in Reno. Within a few days of this announcement, Danny McGhee - the general manager of the Inn - had spoken discretely to Cherylyn, and asked if she would be interested in becoming the senior receptionist, which she was. She had been sad to see her co-worker go, but was also a little excited by the prospect of a new colleague - naively assuming Louisa's post would be filled by someone of similar age.

One week after Louisa had retired, Danny McGhee had walked into reception accompanied by a petite, smiley girl, who would, Danny informed her, be the other receptionist. The younger woman's name was Lisa-Marie; she had the physique of a swimwear model, and looked like she spent a couple of hours perfecting her appearance each day.

Three weeks later, Cherylyn had been reloading paper into the HP printer in the rear office, when she overheard an elderly guest asking Danny if they could speak to the *young, slim receptionist*. Partly out of habit and partly out of naivety, Danny had stupidly called Cherylyn through.

'Hi, there can I help you?' Cherylyn had smiled warmly at the elderly woman, who had frowned in mild irritation back at her.

'No, not *you*, dear,' she had said, as she shook her head. 'I want to speak to that slim, pretty young thing who was working reception last night.'

That had been enough for Cherylyn, who realised she could magnanimously accept her role as the older, larger receptionist, and wear it like an ugly costume, or she could fight to retain her looks and status. She opted for the latter.

The first day on the bike had been easier than she anticipated. It had been her day off, so she rose early, and drove to the Joshua Tree Bicycle Shop where she collected her gleaming purchase. Then, she had returned home, where, after a lunch of Special

K, Cherylyn moved in tentative circles around the backyard of her two-storey home. By 3:00 p.m. she had pulled on the glossy red fibre-glass helmet, and ventured out into the quieter roads. In the weeks that followed, cycling became part of her daily routine - a secret weapon in her war against ageing, and Lisa-Marie's effortless pert little ass.

Cherylyn was three miles out of town, and pushing hard on the pedals, when a sudden noise rose behind her. She turned her head frantically around, and found herself faced with a shuddering wall of metal, as a speeding bus passed dangerously close her. For a scary moment, she felt her bike pulled towards the mass of the dull metal beast thundering past her. It seemed inevitable she would be drawn beneath the wheels of the bus, and crushed to dusty meat. The bike wobbled unsteadily between Cherylyn's legs, but she managed to steady it, as the bus roared away from her.

'Jesus!' she yelled. 'Watch where you're going psycho!' She would have flipped her middle finger to the departing bus, but she was partly unsure if such a defiant gesture would put her further off balance. Instead, she simply put her head down, and continued counting her downward strokes, muttering her annoyance.

It took a couple of minutes before she glanced up and realised the bus had stopped about fifty yards up ahead.

Even though she was already at the limit of her energy, Cherylyn's rage provided her with enough strength to reach the silent vehicle. She glanced up at the dark windows as she moved along the flank of the bus. When she reached the door, she banged angrily on the dark glass.

The door hissed open.

'Listen! I don't know what the hell you thought you were doing back there, but I almost ...' Cherylyn fell silent as she found herself staring down the black barrel of a shining rifle.

'Climb aboard!' the man in the Mickey Mouse hat said, with a fixed grin on his face.

Cherylyn glanced helplessly at the deserted road ahead. The tears fell from her face almost as soon as she stepped off the bike and into the darkness of the bus.

A moment later, a large man in a Hawaiian shirt climbed off the bus and opened the cover of the luggage compartment. He picked the bike up with one hand, and threw it in.

26

The warm mist of the shower filled the cubicle and swirled around Vicki's head. She stood beneath the torrent with one palm pressed against the smooth, charcoal-coloured tiles. She had taken to the bathroom to escape her mother's interrogation about the previous evening. Abigail Reiner was not so easily pacified.

Stepping out of the shower, Vicki wrapped a white towel around herself, turning to find her mother sitting cross-legged on the edge of the bath. In one hand, she held a smouldering menthol cigarette, in the other was crystal ashtray.

'Wow, you gave me a fright.' Vicki tried to sound nonchalant, as she twisted a second towel around her dripping hair.

Her mother sucked on the cigarette, and spoke as she blew the smoke out, 'Who was the man I showed out of my house this morning?'

'What?'

'Don't be obtuse, Victoria. Who was the man?'

'A detective.'

'He claimed you approached him.'

'That's true. Laurie has been missing for some time. I think something bad might have happened to her. I wanted help.'

Vicki, eager to avoid the confrontation, walked out of the bathroom and padded into her bedroom, but her mother merely followed her, hovering in the hallway.

'Are you sleeping with him?' Abigail asked, as she stood in the doorway.

'*What?*'

'You heard.' Abigail crushed the stub of her cigarette into the ashtray. 'Are you sleeping with that old man? He'd obviously spent the night, after your little party.'

Vicki sat on the edge of her bed, where various old photographs of her father remained, scattered like playing cards.

'For god's sake, your sense of timing is great. I've just lost my father.'

'All the more likely it is, then, you would make irrational decisions. Can you imagine how I felt flying three thousand miles to collect your father's insurance documents, and walking in on this?'

'On, what?'

'Your cheap date.'

'I am not sleeping with him, not that it's any of your business.'

'Good, that keeps everything nice and simple, then.'

'What's that supposed to mean?'

'Well, I have informed the police of his intrusion ...'

'His what?'

Abigail's face did not even register her daughter had spoken. She carried on speaking, undaunted by the interruption.

'-and that I would consider any repeat of his visit to represent a criminal act.'

'My friend is missing, possibly murdered, and that kind man is helping.'

'Murdered? Don't be so melodramatic.'

'She is *missing* then,' Vicki clarified, 'and he's helping.'

'Oh, I'm sure he's helping by filling you full of junk food and alcohol?'

'It was me who bought the beer.'

'Oh, jeez, he must have thought he won the state lottery, meeting you.'

'You know, not everyone is a selfish as you!'

'No, of course not. I'm flying back out this afternoon. I appreciate you may be vulnerable, and suitors haven't exactly been thick on the ground, but in my absence, try to avoid inviting any other strangers into my house.'

Abigail turned victoriously out of the doorway, and strode back to the kitchen, leaving her daughter sobbing quietly on the bed. If nothing else, Abigail felt comforted by the fact her daughter would be very unlikely to see the elderly man again.

27

At 2:15 p.m., a couple of lawnmowers were droning sleepily on the opposite side of the street as Leighton sat beneath the yellow parasol at his patio table, with a tall glass of iced tea. He was scribbling methodically on his notepad when a white Punto pulled up in front of the single-storey condo.

'Hi,' Vicki called from the open window, as she leaned across, and smiled sheepishly. She had tortoiseshell sunglasses on her head, and was wearing that faded University of San Diego t-shirt again.

Leighton stepped off the patio, and crossed the shared lawn, dividing the properties from the road. He paused halfway.

'Hey, is your mother waiting in the back-seat with a telephoto lens and a rifle?'

'I'm sorry you had to suffer an encounter with *her*.' Vicki narrowed her eyes, and assumed the icy stare. 'Bitch is as bitch does.'

'Aren't you taking a chance, talking like that?' Leighton smiled. 'She might have followed you?'

'No, she's already headed back to New York.'

'What? I thought she came down to be with you.'

'No,' Vicki scoffed. 'She came to collect Dad's life insurance documents and other paperwork. She's a very efficient woman, you know - even while dealing with the death of her husband.'

'I could see that. So, you want some iced tea, or would that constitute harassment?'

'Well, that would depend on what you've spiked it with.'

'Ah' Leighton smiled. 'Just slices of lemon, I'm afraid.'

'In that case, I'll risk it,' Vicki said, and climbed out of the car.

Leighton went inside to fix her a drink. Vicki sat at the table, and breathed in the sweet smell of the overflowing hanging baskets running along the front of his home. She liked the simplicity of Leighton's world. He seemed to have found a small, comfortable space for himself - self-contained and safe.

'Here you go,' he said, as he placed the glass before her. 'So, did you have any luck with your computer stuff?' Leighton asked, as he sat down.

'Not in terms of a name, but I did find out that the Route King website essentially has no address - it's a stealth parasite page.'

'Oh, that's good.' Leighton nodded sagely. 'But, how about you tell me that in English.'

'It basically sat on the genuine site, then opens a pop-up window in response to a certain stimulus.'

'Stimulus?'

'Yeah, you know, like rolling the cursor over parts of the page, or typing in certain details.'

Leighton thought about this for a moment. A dark thought was forming in his mind. He had already concluded that the bus involved complicit passengers in some way, but he felt that such a unlikely situation couldn't be controlled. There were just too many variables, until he factored in the role of technology.

'Would something like that be able to screen responses to actually target an individual?' he asked.

'In theory, yes.' Vicki said, and took a sip from her glass, 'You think Laurie might have been targeted on purpose?'

'I don't know, maybe.'

'It would be really difficult for a site to target someone on purpose. How would you even know they intended to travel by bus?'

'I'm not sure.' Leighton looked down at his notes for a moment. 'Would it be possible to watch all the people entering their information, and then, you choose when to open the window and offer a better deal?'

A shadow fell over Vicki's face. 'Yeah, yeah, it would.'

'Well, that means that - by screening the bookings, a theoretical killer or killers wouldn't just have to wait for a random victim to pass by in a dark alleyway; instead, they would know exactly where the victim would be, and when. That way the website would basically serve as baited trap setting up the time and place for the killer.'

'Do you know something? It's just that you see more focused.'

'I have a friend who works dispatch in the station. I called her this morning to follow up on a missing police biker.'

'What happened to him?' Vicki asked.

'He vanished whilst working and hasn't shown up for several days. They found his abandoned bike just off route 15. He's not the only one either. Wendy says they have reports of more disappearances coming in every day. She says people have vanished from the roadside or have taken a bus trip.'

Leighton sipped his drink, while Vicki looked intently around at the butterflies dancing from flower to flower in the Californian sunlight.

'That wouldn't happen, though. I mean, snaring strangers to murder? It couldn't ... probably, not really?' Vicki said, trying to restore her sense of order.

'Yet, you personally believe Laurie has been murdered?'

'Well, yes, but not ... you know. It was probably random.'

'When I was a kid, my father was a maintenance man in the Kaiser Steel Mill over in Fontana - have you heard of it?'

Vicki shook her head.

'It was one of the biggest in the world, and to a seven-year-old boy, it was a crazy and exciting old place. Anyway, what I liked best was the nights when my old man would get called out to fix some temperamental motor. He would take me with him - despite my mother's protests - and sometimes, I'd get to the see the bright spray of sparks, as steel was cut, or molten steel being poured like lava.'

'Must've been a dangerous place.'

'A few men died there, crushed between rollers or splattered by a bubble of molten metal. But, that's not why I bring it up.'

'Okay, then, why do you?'

'Because one night, my old man got a call from work, saying there was some kind of crap coming down the cooler wash. This was like a slow waterfall of cold water which cooled the freshly pressed rolls of metal. The operator had called because whatever was in the water was making streaks on the metal. Anyway, the wash was fed by a big tank of the water high up in the roof of the mill. I climbed up two sets of ladders with my old man, and we stood on the gantry. He pressed this grimy switch, and a big old motor slowly rolled back the cover from a square vat of water. I remember it looked like a long, black swimming pool. Anyway, he was kneeling down, holding a jam jar in his hand to take a sample with me holding the torch, when I noticed something bulky and alive moving in the water. I told my pop, and he just pulled a face, and told me to hold the light steady.'

'What was it?' Vicki's eyes widened.

'Well, he dipped his hand back in the water, then he screamed, and fell back on the gantry. His hand was pouring out blood, like a faucet.' Leighton blew out a breath, remembering the scene. 'We got down to the medical room, and found his index fingertip had been torn off. The medical officer drove him to the hospital, where he sat through half an hour of surgery, still ended up looking like he'd put it through a mincer.'

'And where were you when he was being stitched up?'

'Sitting in the reception on a wooden bench, watching the hands ticking by on a big Westfield clock.'

'You must've been terrified, were you?'

'Yeah, well, not as much I was the following morning.' My father insisted on returning to the mill, and we went back up that ladder in the daylight. His hand was bandaged, and he had iodine streaks along his forearm. Up on top, the cover was still rolled back, almost to the edge, and I could see into most of the tank, except this one dark strip down at the end.

'For one crazy moment, I believed he was going to pick up the jar and go dipping again. Only this time, he walked past the bloody jam jar and down to the far end of the tank. I hurried after him, and watched as he gripped a huge drainage tap fixed to the end of the tank, and, despite the pain, he turned it. The water sprayed down on to the steel rolls below, not so much like a stream as water cannon.'

'My father sat back on the gantry, and ruffled my hair. He pulled out a cigarette and smoked as we sat and waited. I couldn't take my eyes of the dark section of the tank. Eventually, the water was low enough that the creature began to panic and thrashed around, before it came out of hiding.'

'What was it?'

'A huge, white Pike - fat and blind. And as long as I was tall.'

'Jeez.' Vicki's eyes widened in horror. 'Did he kill it?'

Leighton chuckled, 'No, my father wasn't the killing type. He probably saw enough of that in Korea. He let me get a good look at it, and he explained how it must have been brought up through the water intake from the Mississippi, and grew for years in the darkness - feeding on anything else that came in through the pipe. He turned off the drain tap and the filler valve, topped it back up, then, he hit the switch, and let the cover clatter back into place.'

'He just left it?'

'Yep, said it was part of nature, it might still be there - they tore down most of the mill, but some of the buildings are intact. But, Vicki, the reason I mention this is because that creature grew there in the darkness, because no one was looking for it. If anyone had suggested to the hundreds of steel-men in the Kaiser Plant a giant white fish swam above their heads year after year, they would have called them crazy. So, I guess what I'm saying is, if you truly hope to find monsters, you first have to be ready to accept that monsters exist. Then, you won't be paralysed with terror when you actually do find them.'

Vicki stared into Leighton's dark brown eyes for a long moment. It was the first time she realised how far she had travelled from the initial shock of thinking Laurie had been murdered to this strange world of darker possibilities.

'Okay,' she finally said. 'What do you really believe is going on?'

'I believe we could have more than one killer.'

'What, like a couple?'

'Yeah, maybe … it's happened in California before,' Leighton said unconvincingly, and looked away.

'But, clearly, you don't think so. What are you not telling me?'

'It could be more than just one or two,' Leighton said, and drained his glass.

'Okay, enough with the vagueness. How many are we talking about?' Vicki demanded.

'Well,' Leighton sighed. 'How many seats are there on a coach?'

'I'm not sure - twenty-eight plus the driver?'

'Then, we're possibly looking at twenty-seven killers on a mobile crime scene.'

Vicki's face paled, and she felt much as she had done on the day her parents had shared their secret divorce.

'How is that even possible? I mean, could there even be that many in the entire country?'

Leighton nodded slowly. 'It varies year to year, but the FBI estimate at any given time there are roughly fifty serial killers active in North America.'

'How do you know?'

'Back in 2009, a bunch of us from Homicide were given a presentation by two agents at Oceanside Precinct. They revealed something called the Highway Serial Killer initiative.'

'What was that?'

'Something dreamt up by the Bureau. It involves a small office in Washington, where a bunch of analysts gather info on victims and suspects, hoping to locate some of those fifty. They hold details on hundreds of murder victims.'

'And you didn't connect this to Laurie's disappearance?' Vicki's voice raised to a crescendo.

'No, most of the victims were either prostitutes or addicts. People with what the feds call a "high risk lifestyle." I don't think your friend falls into that category. She had a steady job, her own home, and no history of substance abuse.'

'And yet, she became a victim. So, what's different now?'

'Perhaps the potential killers are no longer interested in "high risk lifestyle" victims who will be less likely to be missed. Many serial killers were thought to be possibly truck drivers, because the remains of so many victims were found near major routes. The people reported missing in Oceanside seem to match the location profile.'

'My God, why don't the public know about this?'

'At the time, it was never publicised outside of official circles. But, now, the information is out there for anyone who's interested, the thing is, no-one really wants to know. Believing in monsters makes it kind of hard to sleep at night. I should know. You start to listen to every noise, wondering if that creak outside the bedroom door was the cat, or some guy with a long blade and roll of tape.'

'We have to stop them,' Vicki said, with a sense of dawning horror. 'Or at least try to.'

28

It had taken less than three hours for Leighton's small dining room to be transformed into a crude investigation headquarters. A creased old California road map, weighed down in each corner by a bottle of Gold Peak Iced Tea, had replaced the table cloth. Leighton had used silver dollars to mark Barstow and Oceanside.

'Okay,' he said, 'our next step is?'

'We should look at a missing persons' website.'

'I don't have a computer,' Leighton said in an apologetic voice. 'Sorry.'

'It's okay. I have my iPad on the back seat of my car.'

Vicki vanished out of the door, letting a breath of warm night air sweep through the apartment.

She returned a moment later with a glowing tablet gripped securely in her hand. Vicki then perched on the edge of the sofa, and began tapping her fingers purposely on the small screen.

'Type in NAMus,' Leighton suggested. 'There are others, but that one should provide the most detail.'

Vicki looked up at him accusatively. 'I thought you were technophobic?'

'Yeah, but I'm not an idiot. We had to use basic websites to do our job.' Whilst Vicki followed his instructions, Leighton wandered into the kitchen.

'Okay.' Vicki glanced back at the screen. 'I have the site opened here. How should we search them?'

'Geographically, then by date, descending from the day Laurie vanished,' Leighton said, as he returned with a glass jar of silver coins taken from a cupboard in the kitchen.

'I thought we could use a coin to mark each case.'

'Sure,' Vicki said, with a small shrug.

As Leighton unscrewed the lid of the jar, Vicki tapped on the device again, then her eyes widened. 'God, I never realised there were so many.'

'Welcome to America,' Leighton said in wry tone.

'Okay,' she said, 'get to the map.'

'What have you got?'

'Female, aged twenty-four?'

'Last known location?'

'Needles.'

Leighton placed a silver coin on the map, 'Okay, next?'

'Male, thirty-one,'

'Location?'

'Laughlin.'

As Leighton placed the third coin on the map, the doorbell rang, and he instinctively turned his head in alarm. No-one ever came calling on him after business hours. He glanced at his jacket draped over one of the dining chairs. His holster was concealed beneath it like a sleeping pet.

'It's okay. I'll get it.' Vicki grinned.

'What?' Leighton made to stand up, but she hurried by him, patting him reassuringly on the way.

There was a murmur from the hallway, then Vicki returned carrying two flat cardboard pizza boxes.

'What's this?'

'I reckoned it was my turn to buy you dinner,'

'Nice thinking. When did you phone?'

'I didn't. I ordered them on my pad, old timer. Now, we have one Margherita and one Veg Deluxe, You happy to share?'

'Definitely. I suppose advancing technology has some benefits. Like sending Frankenstein to the drive-thru?' Leighton laughed at his own silliness, and fetched some plates from the galley kitchen. Then, because the table was taken, they sat on the floor of the dining room, and shared the warm food.

'So,' Leighton said, as he pulled a triangle of pizza out of the box, 'we have three missing persons, within a thirty mile radius, over, what, a four week period.'

Vicki nodded. 'Is that unusual, I mean, from a cop perspective?'

'Well, from a *cop perspective*,' Leighton narrowed his eyes to convey mock meanness, 'I think it's pretty unusual. Unless that thirty-mile radius happens to cover somewhere with a high population density, like New York.'

'If it's significant, what's our next move? Should we go report it now?'

Leighton thought of his ex-boss and how receptive he would be with him showing up at the precinct with the woman he was accused of harassing.

'No, I doubt they'd care. Firstly we need to find out if any of these other missing persons took a trip on a silver bus.'

'But the site's is dead. How do we find out?'

'Ah, that will require good old fashioned police methods.'

Vicki frowned. 'You mean, we need to eat doughnuts and ignore abductions?'

'I mean, we could go to the last place they were seen, and speak to friends and family.'

'We?'

'Yeah - people respond better to questioning from a male-female team.'

'Ah, so I'm a prop?' Vicki said, as she separated a couple of slices fused together by melted mozzarella.

'An entertaining prop, but I'll cover your lunch, only this time, we take the train.'

'Like I did on the last trip?' Vicki couldn't help reminding him, but smiled when she saw Leighton's expression shift to guilt.

'Hey,' he said, moving to get up, 'you want a beer to wash down that pizza?'

'Sure, that it be great,' Vicki said, but then realised he had only eaten one slice of pizza to her five. 'It's okay, Leighton – I'll get it. You stay there, and catch up.'

Vicki wandered through to the neat kitchen, and was intimidated by the range of copper pans and utensils neatly suspended around the place. She opened the refrigerator, and pulled out two bottles of Coors.

'Where's your bottle opener?' she called.

'In the drawer, next to the icebox,' Leighton replied, sounding like he was chewing.

Glancing down, Vicki found there were drawers on either side of the refrigerator. Rather than disturb Leighton's eating again, she decided to make an educated guess. Opening the drawer on the right side of the icebox, she immediately regretted it. A selection of overlapping photographs lay in front of her. They provided multi-coloured snapshots of a lost life - the four year old girl standing on a faded lawn next to her kneeling father, he in uniform, and she wearing his hat; her first day of school, waving to the camera from the window of the yellow school bus; a blurry Christmas morning, with a girl standing in *The Lion King* pyjamas and clasping a stuffed lioness; a smiling ten year old holding a tin cup, with red ribbons attached to it. One of the most crumpled photographs was of a small girl gently cupping her hands to hold a small falcon. Her eyes were wide with wonder and concern. Beside the pile of photographs were two bottles of Zolpidem sleeping pills. One of them looked half empty. Closing the drawer, Vicki felt like an intruder.

When Vicki came back into the room, and looked at Leighton sitting cross-legged on the wooden floor, eating a sliver of pizza, and peering intently at the screen of her iPad, Vicki felt a sudden of rush of emotion. This quiet, dignified man, who listened to blues and kept a tidy house, was helping her messed up mission, when he had enough hidden pain of his own to deal with. Part of her wanted to thank him somehow - to make it better.

She crossed the room, and sat on the floor purposely next to Leighton, handing him one of the beers.

'Look at this,' he said, tilting the screen so Vicki could see it. 'There are others missing here who were from all over the country but were last seen along the Route 66. The devil's in the detail.'

'How many more are there?'

'Looks like another seven,' Leighton said, as he dragged his hand over the scrub of grey stubble on his face.

'You want me to lay the coins on the map?' Vicki asked.

'Sure, grab the jar, and I'll call them out to you'

By the time the pizza was finished, and the two bottles of beer drained, Vicki and Leighton sat on opposite sides of the table, looking at a scattering of silver coins peppering the map in a roughly rectangular pattern. The shape stretched like a fractured speech bubble from Riverside northwards, then east to Needles, then south through Lake Havasu City, then west to Blythe, and back along to Riverside again.

It looked to Leighton as if the sites marked out a simple, circular route. Most serial killers would produce a map of victims more chaotic than this one. It therefore seemed the regularity of the pattern was down to the specific journey taken by the bus. This meant it was conceivable there were two or three killers out there. A private bus would provide access and opportunity to victims.

'What are you thinking?' Vicki asked.

'About the criminals.'

'What about them?'

'They will most likely be organized, non-social...'

'How do you know?'

'Well, a disorganised killer leaves a trail of chaos from opportunistic attacks; an organised killer is careful. Their trail is neat and tidy, latex gloves, controlled violence, and the victims are preselected. This map doesn't suggest chaos.'

'Well, if you're right, could they just stop what they're doing, vanish back into the world?'

'It's unlikely - most of them only stop in one of three instances - they either get caught - which happens less than most people imagine - or, more often, they kill themselves. That allows them to retain their sense of control right till the end.'

'Or?'

'Huh?'

'You said there were *three* instances. What's the other one?'

Leighton pinched the bridge of his nose, hoping to hell Gretsch was right, and this was just a dumb fantasy. 'They sometimes burn themselves out in a final frenzy. This,' he said, and nodded at the thirty-two coins on the table, 'might only be the warm up act.'

'We should inform someone.'

'I already tried to call it in officially. They won't listen.'

'Why not?'

'I screwed up a few years back.' Leighton sighed, and pinched the bridge of his nose again. 'That's how I ended up working homicide.'

'I thought you moved because of your daughter's accident.'

'It was partly the reason. The night Annie died, I was first at the scene. Nice twist of fate, huh?'

Vicki put her hand on his.

'It's stupid how the stuff you want to forget stays with you the most. The rain was battering down, and it was dark. Danny stayed in the cruiser, calling the accident in. I remember hurrying over the wet road to this small red Honda, and how I had to shield my eyes against the flames coming from the cracked engine ...'

'Leighton, you don't need to tell me.'

'It's okay, you should know. At first, I didn't realise it was her car, but as I got closer, I saw the license plate. I just remember screaming her name, and pulling in the door handle. Got this in the process.' Leighton turned over his right hand, revealing shiny patches of white skin where the pads of his fingers had been fused to the hot metal.

'The smoke was too thick to see inside, but I knew she was already gone. I pulled the door open, but I just made it worse - the rush of air sent the flames into an inferno. The blast knocked me off my feet. But, I saw her, in those seconds before the fire took her. It would have been better if I'd been the one who stayed in the cruiser. She was already dead, but still seated - her legs and hair already on fire.'

'Leighton, I'm sorry.'

'Danny had to drag me away. I was hitting out at the poor guy, but he saved my life. The fuel tank blew, and the force of it slammed us both off the side of our cruiser. They wanted me to take the entire month off, but I had nothing else to do.'

'You went back to work?' Vicki struggled to hide the horror in her voice.

'I did. And things were manageable for a couple of months, until that Sunday afternoon, when we came across a crushed SUV on the freeway. It had hit a patch of diesel and spun out. The driver was inside, banging on the glass. Danny was out of the cruiser in moments, but I couldn't move. He was yelling to me for help, trying to pull the door open.'

Leighton paused, as he became consumed by his own dark memories.

'Did he die?'

'No.' Leighton shook his head. 'Danny got around the passenger side, and pulled him out that way. He was a good cop. After that, I was a pariah in Highway Patrol. Nobody wanted to work with me, and I couldn't blame them, either. Anyway, that's how I got transferred to homicide, but the force occupies a small world, and my reputation reached Homicide before I did. Most of the guys thought I was some kind of unwanted burden to drag around murder scenes with them.'

'That must've been tough.'

'Yeah, for me, and them. But, I'm a decent worker, and I slowly got results earned some respect ... I think that pissed Gretsch off even more.'

'Gretsch?'

'The chief at Oceanside, and my boss for seven long years. He's a determined career cop, who resented my presence there from the start. That was the reason I got pushed to retire early.'

'You mean, it wasn't your choice?' Vicki asked, her eyes widening.

Leighton shook his head. 'A few months back, Gretsch invited me into his office. He put his feet up on the desk and his hands behind his head. He smiled, and asked me how things were going. I remember noting it was the first time the man had ever smiled at me.'

'What did you say to him?'

Leighton shrugged. 'I said while dealing with murder could never really be described as enjoyable, I liked my job, and felt I had helped solve a number of cases, including the Black Mountain Ranch fiasco and one in Morro Hills that got him the promotion to chief.'

'Morro Hills?' Vicki frowned. 'Not that thing about the meatpacking guy that was all over the news.'

'Yeah, my noble chief got the credit for that one.'

'What did he say, in the office, I mean?'

'He said I had got lucky on that case, that I was over the hill, and my pyro-phobia made me liability.'

'What an asshole.'

'I asked what my options were. He told me I could choose to retire, or he could initiate a psych assessment and competency requirement. He already had the papers drawn up for either eventuality. He had them rubber-stamped and ready to go.'

'What did you do?'

'I signed the application for early retirement, and I left.' Leighton sighed.

'Why didn't you fight it?'

'The system's bigger than one pain in the ass.'

'But, surely, you could have done *something*!'

'Maybe,' Leighton said softly, but did not sound like he believed it. 'I guess I just didn't fancy having some stranger taking a walk through my head.'

The beeping noise from Vicki's tablet broke the tension with a shrill alert. She swept her finger across the screen, and tapped an icon to life.

Frowning as she read the text, Vicki turned to Leighton. 'It's an email from a full-time hacker I know from my student days. I asked her to dig into any data linked to the phrase Route King – she's scraped up the name and address of the person who set up Route King's site - and it's local.'

'Looks like the train trip's off,' Leighton said, and got slowly to his feet.

29

At 7:45 a.m. the bright sun was already rising on the car that pulled to a gentle stop outside the two-storey apartment block in a residential area of Midway. The air being drawn through the car's air conditioner carried the greasy stench of frying meat mixed with cigarette smoke.

'Okay.' Leighton turned to Vicki, as he switched off the engine. 'What's your name?'

'Officer Sarah Anderson,' she said resolutely.

'Where's your badge?'

Vicki pulled the jacket of her dark trouser suit open to reveal a metal star in a leather wallet folded over her waistband. She had to wear it that way, because the other side of the badge, pressed against her stomach, revealed a dated photograph of Leighton in his Highway Patrol uniform.

'Excellent.' Leighton smiled. 'Now, remember, this might be nothing, but he could be dangerous. Don't say anything, unless you have to - impersonating an officer is a criminal offence, but can't be proved if you don't actually speak. Just take out the notepad, and write down anything you think important. Okay?'

Vicki smoothed her hair back. For the first time in weeks, absurd as the situation was, she finally felt she was helping to find Laurie.

'Right, then. Let's speak to the man,' Leighton said, and climbed out of the car.

The scuffed door of the apartment was opened by a short scruffy man in his early twenties. His hair was sticking up, and he was wearing three quarter length pants and a faded Pacman t-shirt.

'Mitchell West?' Leighton asked, as he slid one foot into the doorway - ensuring it could not be closed.

'Yeah,' the young man yawned. This was something Leighton had come to associate with guilty people - attempting to appear so relaxed they were sleepy.

'I'm Detective Jones.' Leighton held up his badge. 'This is Detective Anderson. May we come in?'

'What?'

'We have some questions we'd like to ask you,' Leighton spoke slowly. 'To avoid your neighbours hearing, and perhaps drawing a false impression of you, I suggest we speak inside?'

'Yeah, sure,' the young man said. He tried, unsuccessfully, to remain sounding casual, as he ran a hand through his tangled hair.

Leighton noticed before he turned to lead them inside their host had glanced momentarily at Leighton's belt, where his Glock 17 was located. He made a mental note to keep his body out of the other man's reach.

The young man led his visitors through to a sparse living area consisting of bare orange walls, a black sofa, and a wooden table, on which sat a can of Sprite, a half-empty glass, and a tin ashtray with the remnants of a joint in it. West wandered over to the table, and picked up the glass.

'So, what's this about?' he said, taking a small sip of juice.

'You design websites?'

'Yeah, I do a bit. Not a crime, is it?' He raised his chin, as if to challenge Leighton.

The older man was not intimidated and continued with his questions. 'What do you know about a website for a company called Route King?'

West frowned, and moved his eyes upwards in a deliberate thinking pose. 'No.' He shook his head. 'That name doesn't ring any bells.'

'That's strange,' Vicki said. 'Because the Regional Internet Registry has verified that the named person who originally registered the domain name for Route King,' she checked her black notepad, 'is one Mitchell Webster, which we have discovered is the alias you have used to purchase thirty domains.'

Leighton stared at West, hoping to hell Vicki knew her stuff.

'So,' Leighton said steadily, 'I'll ask you again. What you know about the Route King website?'

In one frantic gesture, the young man threw the glass and its contents into Leighton's face, and darted towards the open door. Whilst Leighton clutched his stinging eyes, Vicki grabbed out at West. He responded by thrusting a half made fist into her face, knocking her to the floor. As he broke away from her, he punched Leighton in the kidneys, then vanished out of the room. Leighton staggered against the sofa, gasping for air, then, somehow, righted himself.

'You okay?' Leighton blinked at Vicki, while rubbing his eyes.

'I'm fine,' she lied, and waved a hand at him, holding her bleeding nose with the other.

'Okay, I'm going after him.'

Leighton stumbled out of the door into the bright street, to see West roaring by on a dark green motorcycle. He got a note of the first part of the license plate, but it shrank away from him too quickly. In his younger years, he would have been faster, better. He cursed his naïveté.

Back inside, he found Vicki standing in the small a bathroom, holding a bunched-up handful of toilet tissue against her nose. She looked smaller and more vulnerable here in the dark corners of the real world.

'He's gone.' Leighton breathed out. 'I'm sorry for bringing you here, getting you hurt. I should've come alone.'

'It's okay,' Vicki said. 'You want to take a look around?'

'Hell yes. Whatever his role is in all of this, he certainly wasn't keen on sharing anything, was he? I'll let you get cleaned up.'

As he walked out of the bathroom, Leighton unclipped his Glock - just in case West decided to return. There were two doors outside the bathroom. Leighton pushed open the first on to reveal a cramped kitchen, where Domino's pizza boxes were neatly stacked on the floor, in an angular column, next to a bin overflowing with soda cans.

Proceeding to the second door, Leighton slowly opened it gun first and discovered a room that was both bedroom and workplace. The single bed was neatly made with a white bedding set. Opposite this were two computers and a range of neat black devices lined up on a wooden desk. The screen of the computer furthest away revealed a low budget sex movie, featuring a woman handcuffed to a bed. Leighton discretely moved over and switched off the machine, before Vicki came in. He turned his attention to the desk drawers, all of which were empty.

'You found the set-up?' Vicki asked from the doorway.

'Yeah.' Leighton smiled. 'Seems a bit of a small operation. How's the nose?'

'Blood's dried up. You want me to grab any of the technology? I could use it to get us closer.'

'Yeah, I reckon we're due it as compensation,' Leighton said, 'but let's make it quick.' He placed his gun in his shoulder holster, but left the strap off, just in case it was required. Behind him, Vicki quickly disconnected cables.

'Will you be able to *hack* into them? Is that the term?'

Vicki nodded. 'I hope so. But, we need to take it back to my house.' Vicki stacked the two remote drives and a notebook into a neat pile. 'There,' she said in a nasal tone. 'All done.'

'Okay.' Leighton smiled crookedly. 'Let's get the hell out of here.'

30

At 10:00 a.m., National Park Ranger Frank Mankato, who had been cruising the perimeter of the southern tip of the sprawling desert of the Joshua Tree Park, pulled into the dusty picnic area. Even at this time in the morning, the sand-coloured tables were starting to fill up with families having a snack, or preparing their backpacks before a day of hiking on the long, hot trails.

Frank got out of the vehicle, put his wide brimmed hat on, and made his way through the area. He smiled congenially, and said good morning to the scattered patrons. He made small talk with most of them, mainly ensuring they had enough water, hats, and sunscreen. At this time of year, it was not unusual to get a couple of heatstroke fatalities in the park - during Frank's first year on the job, they had had two in one day, when the temperature hit 105 Fahrenheit.

Picking up some scattered food wrappers from beneath the large metal barbecue, he placed them in a bin, and purposely ignored the two female students who were obviously concealing a couple of joints beneath their wooden bench.

Making his way to the edge of the area, Frank unclipped his binoculars from his belt, held them to his eyes, and surveyed the area for any sign of trouble. There were more dangers in the park than heatstroke. Some trails were a less than a meter wide, and featured sheer drops of hundreds of feet.

Maps, and the ability to use them, were also essential - some people chose to mark their path with the endlessly replicated rock formations and cacti as points of reference, only to find they were walking in wide circles until their water run out, and somebody collapsed.

The information points at the entrance and warnings throughout the park provided travellers with advice, both on potential dangers, and on how to signal for help by using mirrors or smoke signals. Despite the many warnings, most people still put dumb hope in their fancy cell phones, which had limited - if any - coverage in the park.

Frank's sweep of the shimmering horizon found no sign of trouble, and he was about to start back towards the car, park when his attention focussed on a strange, dark object located between two large jumping Cholas, about one hundred and fifty yards from the picnic site. Narrowing his eyes, and keeping them fixed on the object, Frank brought the binoculars back up in front of his bronzed face. He had to adjust the zoom, but, eventually, he got a fix. Whatever the object was, it looked too angular to belong out here.

Tilting his hat brim down over his eyes, Frank jumped off the small mesa on which the picnic site was located, and made a small dust cloud as he landed. He walked purposely towards the object, carefully avoiding the aggressive spikes of the jumping cacti, which covered much of the area.

As he neared the object, he discovered it was a battered leather suitcase. It was roughly the size of the one used by Frank and his wife on their annual holiday to Florida. The initial appearance of ripples and small cracks on the surface of the leather suggested the luggage had been exposed to the elements for at least a couple of weeks.

Frank, instinctively brought his hand to his radio, but then, stopped himself. *What would be the point of calling in an abandoned suitcase?* Another ranger on clean-up duty would still have to make the trip out here to recover it, and it seemed unlikely the owner would be returning to collect it. It would make more sense to throw the ugly old thing into the trunk of his car, and drop it off at the Oasis Park Ranger Station when he stopped in for lunch. Crouching down, he grabbed the handle. He had expected the case to be empty, but found it too heavy to move.

Frowning, and with a dawning senses of uneasiness, he glanced back towards the picnic benches, ensuring they were far enough away to remain oblivious. He then grabbed the brass zipper, and swept his hand to the side, opening the case.

The escaping stench of death was so strong it sent Frank reeling back onto the dusty ground. Cactus needles dug into his hands and pierced his trousers.

He should have hurried then, and saved himself from the nightmares that would plague him for years to come. Instead, he stood up, pulled out a white handkerchief from his pocket, and, scrunching it up, placed it over his mouth and nose.

Somewhere in the bright sky above him, a buzzard was circling. Frank walked back over to the case, and used his foot to lift back a triangle of lid. The woman's body had been forced into the case, like a piece of vacuum-packed meat. Grey duct tape had been wrapped around her mouth and eyes. A tattoo in the form of scripted writing stretched across the skin behind her neck. The ranger knew such a feature would hopefully make identifying the corpse easier. He also noted only one of her hands was visible, but all of the fingers had been removed from it. Frank Mankato said a silent prayer, and hoped to hell the girl had died quickly.

31

With the headlight of the motorcycle switched off, Mitchell West could now see the sky above the dusty valley of the Horseman's Centre was vast and sprinkled with pinpricks of stars. The area, which consisted of a eighty acres of oversized rocks and dust also held two open horse show arenas and an undulating BMX track - all of which were deserted by nightfall.

An hour earlier, he had stopped at a Pic N Pump gas station, just outside Apple Valley, where he bought himself a six-pack of beer and made the call to his employers. He then proceeded to drive out of town to the hills at the rear of the Horseman's Centre, where he parked the bike off the road, drank two tins of beer, and watched the sun go down. He then used the plastic binding to hang the remaining four over his handlebars.

Now, as he leaned back on the cracked leather seat of the Honda, smoking a Marlboro, West looked to the heavens, and wondered for a moment about eternity. Although his own personal god was technology, he occasionally wondered how an omniscient deity would look upon his sins. He reassured himself he had not actually hurt anyone directly, and in case God existed - which he doubted - he would be all good. At least that was what the preachers on the cable TV channels said. Hopefully, this single fact would save his soul, when the time came to meet his maker. Not that he was planning on that any time soon.

As he crushed the cigarette under the heel of his boot, West had been so distracted by the relentless whirring and clicking of the native insects he did not notice the large man in the Hawaiian shirt, who stepped softly through the undergrowth towards him, until he was standing beside him.

'Why did you call him?' the large man asked.

'Shit!' Mitchell West shuddered. 'Do you have to sneak up on people?'

'Why did you call?' the large man repeated.

'I got fucking raided.' West said, as he struggled to settle his breathing.

'You what?' The large man frowned.

'A couple of cops came sniffing around my place. They were asking about the site.'

'What did you tell them?'

'Nothing. I told them squat.'

'And they left?'

'Yeah, they left.'

'Why are you here?'

'I left in a hurry. All my shit is back at the house - my computers … everything.'

'Is the website down?'

'No, it doesn't need a physical operator.' West laughed, 'Jeez, man, did you listen to anything I said at the diner?'

'No,' the large man sighed. 'Probably not.'

'The site will tick along just fine. But, the thing is,' West puffed out his chest, 'I'm going to need to, you know, be recompensed?'

'For what?'

'Well, I need somewhere to stay now, and I need to replace the equipment.'

'But, you said the site would be fine.'

'The site will be fine, but I still need a fucking computer. That's how I make my living.'

'You were paid up front.'

'Yeah, but that was before your *activities* drew some unwanted fucking attention, man.'

'You need more money, then, is that it?'

'Yes, fuck, yes! Finally.'

The man in the Hawaiian shirt turned away from West, and looked into the darkness, 'Well, should I?' he called to a darker shadow amongst the oversized boulders.

'Hey,' Mitchell West squawked, suddenly spooked. 'Who the fuck are you talking to, man?'

The large man ignored him, and kept his attention on the darkness, from where a soft single word was spoken.

'Yes,' it said.

'Hey,' West repeated, but by then, the large man had turned back around to face him, jamming a long boning knife deep into Mitch's abdomen. Pulling the blade out, he watched as West looked down in disbelief at the hot, dark patch spreading like ink across his t-shirt. The large man was experienced, and had pushed the knife in far enough to pierce the spleen, guaranteeing West would bleed to death in minutes.

Mitchell West swayed slightly and his hot blood dripped on to the parched dusty ground. The large man walked back to the bike, where he removed one of the beers from the handlebars. Sparking it open, he took a deep gulp, belched, and settled back to watch the show.

32

L eighton stood on the balcony of Vicki's apartment and watched the ocean waves as they crashed in long explosions on the shore. It was a warm afternoon, and the beach was crammed with families. Behind him, Vicki was peering intently at a computer screen. She had been silent for over half an hour. Leighton was lost in his own thoughts, remembering taking his daughter to the beach, where she had dug for pretty shells, and he had read trashy novels. If he could have a second chance to be with her, he would have put down the book and spent more time digging with his child.

'Okay there?' Vicki called to him.

'Sure. How you getting on?' Leighton moved back into the apartment, sat down on the sofa alongside Vicki, and rubbed his hands together.

'Hmm.' Vicki frowned at the screen. 'There's not much data, but what there is generally suggests the site would sit on top of a genuine web page. The imposter would appear genuine in terms of the web address and the appearance, but it would be entirely fake.'

'Like a fake ATM fascia crooks use to scam bank cards?'

'Exactly. Anyway, it would filter the data ...'

'Filter for what?'

'Whatever made the ideal victim - solo travellers, one-way tickets, isolated locations, age, gender ...'

'Okay, so what can we do with this?' Leighton tried to sound hopeful.

'Not a lot,' Vicki admitted. 'But, because the memory had stored the general parameters, I was able to go to various bus companies, and activate the automatic page redirect.'

'What does that mean?'

'I found the only sure-fire way to find the damned bus.'

'And what would that be?' Leighton asked quietly.

'To book a ticket on it,' Vicki said, and met Leighton's eyes.

'No way!' Leighton shook his head.

'Hear me out,' she said, widening her eyes.

'I said no way. Look, Vicki, these are killers - real sadistic bastards. This isn't CSI!'

'I don't need to *physically* get on the bus,' Vicki persisted. 'We just make a booking, and wait out of sight at a bus stop to see if actually shows up. I'll bring a camera - even if it speeds on by, I can get the plates and a shot of the driver, too, maybe.'

'And then what?'

'We follow it at a distance and call your old boss, give them everything we've got'

'Yeah, sure.' Leighton shook his head dismissively.

'You don't agree?' Vicki turned around fully to look at Leighton. 'Then, explain what we should do, Leighton. Otherwise, we're doing nothing!'

'I just think we could explore other options.'

'Like what, stake out every bus stop, and hope we get lucky?'

'It would be a hell of a lot safer.'

'Well, to be honest, it's all academic now, anyway.'

'What's that supposed to mean?'

'I've already booked the ticket.'

'*What?*'

'I got a ticket under a false name for a pick-up from outside Blythe, tomorrow afternoon. A similar bus stop to the one Laurie was picked up from. I was going to use the exact same one, but I reckon that would arouse suspicion.'

'It's not safe. Christ, Vicki, you don't want to put yourself in the lion's den.'

'So, what are we meant to do, Leighton, huh?' Vicki stood up in frustration. 'How the hell do you think we can get these people?'

'I don't know,' he said honestly, a 'but this isn't it.'

'You ever hear that line about how all it takes for evil to succeed is for good people to do nothing? Well, that's what we're doing - nothing!'

Leighton looked shamefully at the ground.

'Look, as long as we waste time eating nice food, and thinking up plans, people are dying! I know you have your demons, Leighton, but this is your chance to save someone else's son or daughter.'

'I know,' he said flatly.

Vicki came over to sit with him and took his hand. 'If you do this, the next time you go to the cemetery and stand by her grave, you won't be so hard on yourself.'

Leighton's gaze met hers.

'I've never been,' he said in a tone of contrition.

'What?'

'I've never been to her ... you know ... the cemetery,' he said quietly. 'I don't want to stand there and make it okay, as if what happened was fair.'

'Do you never feel like going?'

'Yes, I do ... every birthday, every holiday, each time I pass any cemetery or any florist. She loved daisies - those crazy, oversized ones.'

'Then, why don't you?'

'Because I'm not that guy - I wasn't there for her. Hell, I was supposed to keep her safe. And now to go there - to stand on that neat grass, playing the poor grieving father, while my daughter has nothing, seems wrong. Does that make any kind of sense?'

'You're a good father, Leighton.'

'You don't know me.' Leighton shook his head. 'I was average, at best. Even as a kid, there were things she loved, *really* loved. When she was eight years old, I took her over to the Bird Sanctuary in Del Mar, and she got all attached to this little injured Merlin hawk they had there - bright red, it was. We were there the day the rescue team brought it in and she held it so gently. Man, she pestered me every single weekend to go there.'

'Did you go back?'

'Only once or twice, but the Merlin was gone by then. You see – that's the busy kind of dad I was. I bought her a little toy, one she took to bed every night, but by then, I'd already let her down.'

'Nobody's perfect, Leighton - I wasn't the best daughter to my parents, or the best friend to some lonely girl stuck in a dust bowl town with no family, but that doesn't make me label myself as bad and just roll over and quit. It makes me more convinced I owe it to my friend to stop the people who took her life.'

Something in Vicki's eyes convinced Leighton she would not be dissuaded on this one.

'Look,' he sighed. 'If we do this, we need to plan this out. I can call both the Bureau and the station in the morning. I can ask dispatch to let Gretsch know what we're planning to do. Maybe they could send some support. But, if the bus actually shows up, you do not get on it, okay?'

'Of course.' Vicki nodded enthusiastically.

'It might be better if I stood with you.'

'Then, the bus maybe wouldn't stop - all the missing people were travelling alone. Plus, if it slows down long enough for me to make like I'm going to get on, you would still be able to call in the cavalry.'

Leighton turned his head, and looked back towards the ocean.

'If we are going to do this, I want you to be armed. Take my revolver, okay?'

'Sure.'

'You'll be armed, you promise?' Leighton asked quietly.

Vicki nodded. 'I promise. This is the only way we will know for certain.'

'Okay,' Leighton sighed, 'we'll do it.'

33

The night shift in the Midland Truck Repair Centre was thankfully over for Mike Bernal. As he drove his orange truck along the deserted stretch of road from Peoria to Blythe, he was lost in thought. When his radio crackled, and hissed to life he switched it off, and sighed.

Things between him and Janey had been at a low point, and he felt something needed to change. It seemed they rarely spoke, except to exchange functional information, and even these simple conversations seemed to be loaded with unexpressed dissatisfaction.

On some nights, he would go sit in the truck, smoking a cigarette, and listening to the emergency channels on his scanning radio. He knew it was illegal to listen in on those crackly frequencies, but it beat the hell out of cable television. As he sat in the darkness, he often stared at the stars, and visualised whatever drama was unfolding out there on the roads or in the nearby towns.

Mike wondered momentarily about whether he should have brought her flowers, like he had done the previous week. It had worked to the extent the conversation was, at least for the Saturday, less depressing. But, then, to continually bring home gifts to raise the atmosphere to normality would be seem to almost be rewarding her distance. It would possibly just be simpler to ask her what was wrong, but he guessed he already knew the answer to that.

Janey had turned forty years old just two months earlier. He still found her as attractive as ever, but he often found her scrutinising her reflection in the bathroom mirror. He suspected she was lonely. In some respects, he understood it couldn't be easy living in such an isolated property, with no real neighbours for miles, but the secluded bungalow had been her dream house. At least, it had been, at first.

Mike's jeep was rounding the curve of Tom Wells Road, when the speeding bus nearly hit him. The narrow road was neither designed for, nor accustomed to, an intercity bus. It thundered around the corner, taking up most of the middle of the road. The suddenness of the unexpected wall of metal, shuddering towards him, forced Mike to skid on to the dusty verge of the road. This misshapen verge of the road was so strewn with rocks the wheels of the jeep shuddered and threw up a cloud of debris, forcing him to a stop. He swore, as he slammed a fist against the dashboard. Glancing in his side view mirror he found - as expected - the bus was long gone into the cloud it had left in its wake.

Whilst he waited for the dust to settle, Mike pulled a packet of Winston cigarettes out of the glove box, removed one from the pack, and pushed in the cigarette lighter. When it popped, he used it, and blew a grey cone of smoke out. His brief brush with death left him off-centre for a minute. Staring into the dry scrub-land, his eyes fell on the distant Rockies, and he felt the soothing effects of nature. It seemed perhaps more important than ever to get things back on track at home.

Once his rattled state of mind had settled, Mike restarted the engine, and drove off the verge and back on to the road. He drove much more slowly around the next bend he came to. He knew this corner well, as it was located only fifty meters from his home. Perhaps if he had been driving faster, he would not have noticed the thing at the side of the road. This small fact would be something he would think about for years afterwards. But, the slow pace allowed him to catch a glimpse of it - a bright yellow tennis shoe, just like the ones his wife wore. This was not a soft pastel yellow, but rather the screaming bright colour of emergency services. Whenever she wore them around the house, Mike would call her Big Bird or BB for short. *What a strange coincidence*, Mike thought, *that a shoe, just like his wife's, should be discarded in the scrub land so close to their house.*

Mike smiled to himself, and decided he would use this funny fact to break the ice when he got back to the house. He would ask Janey if her shoes had started breeding. Maybe they could take a walk along the verge together, so he could show her the lone shoe. He could tentatively take her hand on the walk back and offer to fix brunch, or they could go out to somewhere nice in Blythe - get back on track together.

Steering into the driveway of his sprawling bungalow, Mike switched off the engine, and stepped out of the jeep.

At the side of the house white, clean clothes were drying on the taught washing line. This sight was always something which reminded Mike of his childhood, and he found inexpressible comfort in the fact Janey was so reliable in her quietly meticulous care of their home.

Opening the screen door, Mike found the inner door was ajar. This did not alarm Mike - on hot days, both the front and rear doors were kept open to allow a through breeze. What did alarm him, however, was the single item of footwear lying in the middle of the hallway.

'Janey?' he called, as he knelt down and picked up the yellow tennis shoe.

There was no reply.

Mike felt an uncomfortable shift of energy inside him, confirming at some primal level something was very wrong. He took the shoe with him, as he hurried back outside into the bright morning light. Clambering back into the jeep, he revved the engine, and sped off in screeching cloud of dust.

When he got the place where he had seen the shoe, Mike pulled up the jeep, switched on the emergency warning lights, and climbed out. The internal part of him already knew what to expect, and was simply allowing his conscious mind to catch up.

As he reached out to the discarded training shoe, Mike picked it up, and held next to Janey's shoe - making a perfect pair. On the recovered shoe, a smear of blood was vividly contrasted against the bright yellow material. He held the two shoes to his stomach, and let out a single sob.

Staring at the dusty roadside in disbelief, he noticed something that broke his paralysis. There were tyre tracks alongside the verge where his wife's bloodied shoe had been lying. Given the fact Mike had spent thirty-one years working as a truck mechanic, he knew the tyre tracks belonged to a bus, and most likely the one that had near run him off the road, seventeen minutes earlier.

Climbing back into his jeep, Mike pulled the glove compartment open again, only this time, he threw the cigarettes aside and removed a 9 mm Cougar pistol. He took the safety off the handgun, started the engine, and slammed the jeep into gear.

34

Abigail Reiner walked through the front door of the beach house, carrying her two items of matching luggage, and closed the door with her foot.

'Victoria – are you in?' she called, and placed her bags neatly against the wall closest to the door.

Despite the fact she had been joint owner - along with her deceased ex-husband - of the house for over a decade, Abigail Reiner felt little emotional connection with the place. Her ex-husband had suggested she was incapable of such a response, but he was wrong. She simply had too many responsibilities to indulge in time wasting emotions. Without her efforts and lack of soul searching, she would not have a successful career, and luxuries such as the beach house could quite simply have never been achieved.

The house felt warmer than she liked it – possibly as a consequence of spending so much time in the fresher environment of the East Coast. Her heels clicked noisily on the tiled floor as she walked over to the wall mounted panel and turned on the air conditioning. She walked through to the living room, and surveyed the place with a critical eye.

Making her way along the hallway to the bedroom, Abigail fully expected to find her over-sensitive daughter to be curled on her bed, hiding from the world. This personality defect in her daughter, which must have been inherited from her father, was what had driven Mrs. Reiner to return to Oceanside for the week. If she allowed Vicki to spend any more time retreating from the world, her career prospects would plummet even further. She called her daughter's name again. There was no response.

Eventually, Abigail walked into the stale air of what had once been her own, beige-coloured bedroom. She crossed the spacious room, and sat on the bed. Reaching down, she opened a small bedside cabinet, and removed a TV controller.

Abigail switched on the wall-mounted television. She then bit on her bottom lip as she selected the designated channel connected to her security camera, and the HD recorder located in her wardrobe.

As she reviewed the car park footage of the previous few hours, Abigail resisted the urge to scream in rage.

Instead, she snapped open her phone, and used a manicured nail to tap a staccato pattern on the screen. Holding the telephone to her ear, she chewed on inside one cheek.

'Hello, police,' a bright voice answered. 'Can I help you?'

'My name is Abigail Reiner. Who is the most senior person in your building right now?'

'I can deal with any report you might wish to make.'

Abigail pulled a face, as if she had bitten into some bitter fruit 'What's your name?'

'Officer Piper.'

'Well Officer Piper, I'm sure you believe that,' she said calmly, 'but let me be blunt. I want to speak to someone more senior than a glorified answering machine about an urgent police matter. If you continue to be obstructive, I will hang up this phone, call my lawyer, and instruct them to start preparing a case for obstruction against you.'

There were a few moments of silence, then a new voice answered the phone.

'Hello, Mrs. Reiner, this is Chief Gretsch. What can I do for you?'

'I called two days ago regarding my daughter being harassed by a retired detective.'

'Yes.' Gretsch sighed audibly. 'And I can assure you, Mrs. Reiner, I personally spoke to the man concerned. He won't be bothering your daughter again.'

'Well, that doesn't inspire me with confidence.'

'Why would that be, Mrs. Reiner?'

'I believe my daughter has been abducted by Jones, and, Chief Gretsch, if this turns out to be the case, and if you do not bring the full weight of the law upon this bastard, I'll see you in court to request your head on a fucking plate.'

35

The woman on the floor of the bus had finally been subdued. Two of the passengers were sitting on top of her, and a third was holding a halothane mask over her red face. All of the remaining passengers were staring serenely out of the bus windows.

The tall, scrawny man holding the mask in place was dripping with sweat. His appetite had put them all at risk. His name was Desmond Dyer, and up until that day, he had been responsible for the murder and sexual assault of no less than thirty-six women - all of them aged between thirty and forty-five, with long dark hair. Three of them had been killed on the bus, two others at the farm in Laughlin.

Forty-two minutes earlier, the bus had been rumbling to an agreed drop off point six kilometres outside Blythe, when it had passed by the garden of a house, where a slim woman with chestnut hair had been hanging washing on a line. Dyer, who was on driving duty, had slammed on the brakes. Some of the passengers had lurched forward.

'What the fuck are you doing, Dyer?' Wendell Stein, a large man in cargo pants and yellow Hawaiian shirt, called out, and waddled down the aisle to the driver.

'Her,' Dyer said softy, and pointed to the woman the garden.

'No way!' Stein narrowed his eyes. 'You know the rules. Bookings only.'

Dyer wasn't listening. His eyes were fully locked on to the woman, as she pegged the clothes on the washing line. Stein recognised the expression of obsessive desire on Dyer's face.

'Hey.' Stein clicked his fingers at him. 'Hey, get back in the room, you crazy bastard.'

Without replying, Dyer had leapt out of the driver's seat, and lurched off the bus.

'Oh shit!' Stein made a grab for him, but was not quick enough.

Janey Bernal was lost in thought about Mike when she was startled by the hissing brakes of the long silver bus stopping opposite her yard. She had been thinking about how maybe they could adopt a child. It seemed such a waste of life, otherwise.

However, when she glimpsed the driver, she felt no alarm - he was probably just lost, and looking for directions.

Dyer hurried excitedly into the yard of the house, and called out to the woman. 'Excuse me, ma'am.'

Janey looked up, holding one hand up to shield her eyes from the sun. 'Can I help you?' she asked.

'Yeah, sure.' Dyer grinned. 'I need you to get on the fucking bus.'

'What?' Janey stifled a shocked laugh.

Dyer pulled a butterfly knife from his rear pocket. 'I'll not tell you twice, bitch,' he said in a dry humourless voice.

Jane made a sudden lunge to the side, and before Dyer could respond, she jumped over the laundry basket, and ran across the yard. Stumbling to the door, she got inside the hallway of house. Gasping for breath, she locked the door behind her, hoping the other passengers on the bus had seen the psychopath's behaviour, and were currently calling the cops. She didn't see the large man in the Hawaiian shirt step out of the kitchen and into the hallway behind her. He grabbed her around the waist, picking her up. Jane kicked and screamed, knocking off one of her shoes in the process, but her efforts were wasted - he was simply too strong. Using his free arm, her attacker opened the front door to find the scrawny man still outside, stepping from side-to-side, like an excited child.

'You need a hand there, Stein?' he said, grinning at the large man.

'I've got her,' he replied angrily. 'Just get back on the fucking bus before anyone sees us!'

The scrawny man did as he was told, but still appeared dangerously excited, as he hurried across the yard. Janey, who had allowed her body to go limp, was simply playing possum. As the man carried her across the yard, she remembered something from her high school self-defence class. She balled one hand into a solid fist, then slammed it backwards, as hard as she could, into the man's groin. He groaned in agony, and momentarily released her. That was all Jane needed. She broke away from him, and burst into a sprint. No longer trusting the house, she ran sideways out of her yard, and into the scrub-land parallel with the road.

The large man yelled out in pain and rage, then began pursuing her through the dusty countryside. Janey stumbled frantically over rocky terrain, wearing only one shoe, and cutting her bare foot on sharp rocks and cactus spines. She knew her attackers wouldn't want to be seen, so perhaps, if she made it to the road, she could flag down a car.

Despite his bulk, Stein was fast, and caught up with her, just as she reached the road. He threw his bulk against Janey's back, knocking her to the ground. Standing up, her grabbed her by the hair, and yanked her towards the now approaching bus. She screamed in response to the burning pain ripping across her scalp.

As Stein clambered aboard, dragging the squealing woman behind him, he stopped on the final step, and looked straight at Dyer, who was grinning in the driving seat, then punched him fully in the face, bursting his lip like a squashed pink slug.

'You put everything at risk, you selfish prick. You can take her to the house, but I have a booking in an hour. If you're not finished with your cougar by then, I'll gut and skin the both of you. Now, get the fuck out of that seat, and deal with her!'

He threw the woman on to the aisle of the bus. She was nothing more than an inconvenience to him. Unlike Dyer, he only liked natural blondes, and they had to be clear-skinned and aged between fourteen and twenty-five - give or take. Dyer pushed past Stein, and wiped the blood from his month.

'Can somebody get the halothane, please?'

Stein put the bus in gear, and it lurched finally forward again.

36

At 2:33 p.m., Gretsch was finally getting some lunch. As he leaned over the paper bag on his desk and bit into the turkey and bacon sub, he tried to formulate a potential strategy. The shit-fest surrounding Leighton Jones and his delusion about an imaginary bus full of serial killers, was starting to impact on the real world.

For most of the previous hour, Gretsch had been locked in a heated conversation with Agent Andrew Donaldson, from the Bureau, who wanted to know why a recently retired Oceanside detective had contacted Quantico that morning to report a group of suspected serial killers active in California. He was particularly curious about the fact there had been no indication of such suspicion from any police station in any of the state's major cities.

Donaldson had said, in a deliberately accusative manner, this generated two equally alarming possibilities. The first was there was a fantasist ex-cop, running around sharing all sorts of wild claims with national agencies; the second was three thousand police officers across two states had failed to notice a mobile nest of serial killers operating in their own back yards.

It had taken some time, but Gretsch had gone through Leighton's history with Donaldson, explaining he was generally considered unstable and should be ignored. He, of course, made no reference to the incident at Black Mountain Ranch, in which Leighton had saved both his chief's life and his career. Instead, Gretsch painted a picture of depressive cop, with an unhealthy fixation on a vulnerable young woman.

The bus story was, he suggested, probably just something Jones had invented to keep the girl scared, and therefore, interested.

Donaldson listened in ambiguous silence then suggested Gretsch should formulate a strategy to deal with the situation a little more effectively.

As he hung up the phone, Gretsch leaned back in his chair and stretched. He had taken a single sip of now cold coffee and a second bite of his sandwich, when there was an abrupt rap on the office door, which opened, and Officer Lusk entered, holding a sheet of A4 paper in front of him like a thin shield.

'Sir, I'm sorry to interrupt your lunch, but think you should know about this.'

'Okay.' Gretsch wiped at his mouth with a white handkerchief. 'What is it?'

'Well, it relates to this business with Leighton Jones.'

'There's a fucking surprise.' Gretsch belched, and waved his hand dismissively. 'Go on.'

'Yesterday morning, we took a call from a guy called Coombs, whose elderly mother was due to arrive in San Francisco on Monday, only she never showed up.'

'So what? Elderly folks regularly go walkabout every day.'

'He called his mom's neighbour and asked him to check. The neighbour confirmed the house was locked up, and said he saw Mrs. Coombs leave.'

'Is that it? You interrupt my brief fucking lunch for that?'

'Wait, there's more. Mr. Coombs also said he booked his mother on to a new bus service. Got the ticket himself on-line. Anyway, he said when he tried to call the bus company to see if the lady got on the coach, the company doesn't seem to exist.'

Gretsch narrowed his eyes, and pushed the remainder of his sandwich away. He then sat up, placed his elbows on the desk, and pushed his fingers together.

'Anything else?' he asked, in a slightly more concerned tone than before.

Lusk nodded.

'This morning, we got a call from Detective Steve Abornazine up in Laughlin. He's following up a missing person report on one

Joanne Palmer - a twenty-five-year-old female, who apparently boarded a bus to San Diego, and never showed up at her destination either.'

'Any witnesses see her get on this bus?'

'Yeah, her boyfriend, apparently. He was the one who called it in.'

The colour began to drain from Gretsch's face.

'That's not all,' Lusk continued nervously. 'Dispatch received a call from a man over in Blyth, who believes his wife was abducted this afternoon. He reported seeing, I quote, "a large, silver bus" in the vicinity at the time, and he believes it may be involved.'

'Shit!' Gretsch took his head in his hands.

'Then, a couple of minutes ago, we got this call from Leighton Jones.'

'What did he say?'

'That he's staked out a bus-stop, where he believes the suspect vehicle will show up. He's requesting back-up.'

'Did he mention having anyone else with him?'

'Yes.' Lusk checked his notepaper. 'Vicki Reiner. He said she had made a booking on the bus.'

'What did you tell him?'

'I haven't answered. He's still on the line out there.' Lusk glanced back towards the reception area.

'He's on the line right now?'

'Yeah, I didn't want to respond without speaking to you.'

'Okay, tell him that we are keen to help, and we'll send assistance to support him. Then, dispatch a cruiser with the instructions to arrest Jones, and bring the old bastard in!'

'What do we charge him with?'

'Everything we can!'

After Lusk left the office, Gretsch groaned, picked up his coffee mug, and threw it at the wall, where it exploded into white porcelain shards.

37

Leighton sat in his car sweating on the opposite side of the road from Vicki who stood nervously at the bus stop. His car was pulled back from the road, partly concealed between two empty shells of buildings, but still having a clear view of the bus stop.

The former detective was nervous as hell. Firstly, he was concerned for the safety of the girl standing at the bus stop, and occasionally waving a discreet hand at him. In many ways, he felt the plan was flimsy as hell, and yet, he cared enough for Vicki to go along with it. She was right, too - this was the closest they had come to seeing if the damned bus even existed. Secondly, he knew he had already broken a number of laws to even get this far, and his phone call to the station had done little to reassure him.

An unfamiliar officer had taken the call. They had sounded initially dismissive, and then alarmed, as Leighton explained what he and Vicki were planning to do.

Eventually, after some dead time on the line, when the officer went to check with a more senior officer, they had agreed to send some type of assistance. Now, alone in his car, without the comfort of a valid police badge, Leighton hoped to hell they hadn't been lying.

After a smattering of cars and trucks passed them, the silver bus finally appeared on the horizon, shimmering in the heat-haze of the road. Leighton watched intently as Vicki held up one hand to shield her eyes from the scorching sun, and used the other to wave to the bus. While this happened, a reflected glint of sunlight from the bus bounced off something on the floor of Leighton's car. The flash of light caught his eye, and he glanced down to see the revolver he had given to Vicki was half concealed. As he reached down to recover the weapon, the bus pulled up to the stop, blocking Leighton's view.

'Shit!' He reached down fumbling to reach the weapon. 'Hey, Vicki!' he called, and clambered out of the car.

At that moment, there was a loud whoop as a police cruiser appeared from nowhere and screeched to a stop in front of Leighton's car, blocking it in. For a moment, Leighton felt relief, as he stupidly assumed that the officers had arrived to deal with the bus, but this notion was quickly dispelled when two officers tumbled from the car and pointed their guns towards him rather away from him.

'Drop the weapon, Jones!' the taller of the two officers shouted at him.

'Wait, that's the bus I called about...'

'Drop the fucking weapon, or I *will* shoot.'

Caught between confusion and panic, Leighton let the revolver fall to the ground, and held his hands up. One of the officers, a tall lean man called John Ross, hurried to him, grabbed Leighton by the wrist, and twisted it, turning him around, and slamming him against his car.

'Listen,' Leighton tried. 'You've got to list-'

Leighton felt his feet kicked apart. Someone grabbed his head, and his hands were roughly pushed together and cuffed. He twisted his face to look towards the bus, which was pulling away. When the silver bulk had passed, Leighton found, as he expected, the bus stop was empty.

'Leighton Jones, I am arresting you on suspicion of trespass, theft, and the abduction of a vulnerable person. You have the right to remain silent, you have the right to an attorney ...'

He didn't hear the rest. All of his mental processes were consumed by the horror of Vicki's situation, and the fact she was aboard the fleeing bus, unarmed.

38

Janey opened her eyes; the left one was painful and swollen. She tried to reach for it, and instantly felt a flash of pain rip across her shoulder. It was then, in those first moments awake, that she realised the absolute horror of her situation. She was naked and fastened, with a pair of steel handcuffs which were looped through the centre bar of the headboard of a rusting metal bedstead. Her head was propped up on a shapeless pillow. Beneath her body, the stained mattress was wrapped in clear plastic. The room was old with a scarred wooden floor and peeling floral wall paper. To her left, was the only source of watery light - a grimy window. But, perhaps worse than all of these discoveries, was the fact a piece of duct tape had been wrapped around her head, covering her mouth. She barely had time to recall the horror of her abduction, before she heard footsteps outside the door.

Janey genuinely flinched as the door opened, and the tall man, who had dragged her to the bus, walked in. His right hand was clamped around what she initially thought was a rifle, but as he approached, she saw it was some type of plastic tripod.

'Well, hi there, miss.' He grinned at her. 'I hope you had a nice rest. Soon, you're going to need your energy.'

For a painfully long time, the man simply stood staring at Janey, drinking in her naked vulnerability. He loved this part of his ritual, almost more than the later, messier stuff. At this point, he was fully in control - he was the one with the power over the bitch that had attracted him.

He then began to whistle to himself, as he assembled the black metal tripod, and placed it on the ground at the foot of the bed.

'You might be saying nothing just now, but you'll be so noisy later on. That's why I have these.' He began to rummage around in his trouser pockets, producing two grubby foam earplugs, which he held out triumphantly. Janey could not think beyond the horrifying fact that the sadistic man, who was arranging to rape and murder her, looked so ordinary. There was no scarred deformity, no villainous laugh - just a bland man, like millions of others.

'Now,' he said, no longer looking at her, 'I'm just going to fetch the old video camera from the barn, so don't you go rushing off anywhere.'

He left the door open intentionally, as if to mock his chained-up victim with the illusion of escape.

In response to this, Janey fought an insistent urge to whimper herself into despair. Part of her mind was almost defeated by the absolute horror of her predicament, and yet, something inside her refused to let this pathetic man have any dominion over her. Instead, she focussed on the one moment of good fortune in the entire nightmare.

As a child, Janey had saved scavenged pennies in an old jam jar, which she secretly kept in the musty shadows beneath her bed. One rainy February afternoon, she had tipped them out on to her Snow White bedspread to count them. They had all clattered into a metallic puddle on the bed, except for one of the stubborn coins that remained stuck to the bottom of the glass jar, adhered by the remnants of the original jam.

Janey had pushed one of her hands into the jar to release the coin, with the ragged nail of one small fingertip, only once her knuckles and thumb joint were in past the rim, her hand got stuck. Reluctant to break the jar, for fear of being cut, Jane had twisted her hand with the strange glass glove. Finally, in a moment of inspiration, she moved her thumb across the palm of her hand, and felt a weird inaudible click as it dislocated. Her hand had moved instantly free of the glass prison. In the ensuing years, she had practised this move many times. She would often help her mother around the home, by recovering items dropped into small places.

Now, in the abyss of her desperate situation, Janey knew she had one small chance of escape. However, this was dependent on her ability to stay entirely in the moment.

Janey twisted her head around to look at the headboard. Moving her hands slowly forward and backwards a couple of times, she performed the simple act of dislocation and pulled first one hand and then the other through the handcuffs. Her main concern was to stop the handcuffs from falling and clattering noisily on to the floor. She managed to prevent this from happening by pressing the metal hoops firmly against the back of her head, until she was able to move them on to the mattress.

Her wide eyes scanned the desolate room for any type of potential weapon. She spotted a bedside cabinet and opened the drawer, carefully trying to suppress the dull scrape of wood on wood. Inside was a blood-smeared roll of duct tape, a small Kodak camera, and a long boning knife.

Janey felt a flicker of hope ignite inside her. She held her breath, removed the knife, and placed it under the pillow. Aware that keeping the handcuffs in place would simply be too difficult, Jane let them slip down beneath the knife. She then shifted her body painfully up the bed, and placed her hands above her head, in the position they had originally been fastened. She adjusted her sweating hands so they gripped the knife handle, and tried to avoid thinking about its dry, crusty texture.

When the man returned with the camera, he clipped it onto the tripod and switched it on, and Janey heard the motor groaning to life. A small, red LED light blinked steadily beneath the eye of the lenses. The man looked at Janey, and ran his tongue over his bottom lip. What he did next was even more unsettling, he turned to the camera, held up two thumbs in a gesture of success and turned back to her.

'Now, we are going to have some fun, bitch, and, if you're a good girl, I've got a nice surprise in the drawer for you.'

He pulled off his t shirt and pants to reveal his skinny, pasty body before he climbed up on to the bed. He grabbed Janey's legs, forcing them apart and knelt between them. She noticed his small erection was stabbing at the material of his underwear.

'It's time to play.' The man grinned.

As her attacker hooked his two thumbs into the waistband of his underpants, Janey seized her chance. Springing forward, she drew the knife in both hands from behind her head, and thrust it directly into the man's throat. He let out a strange meowing noise, and tried to clamber away. His blood felt unnaturally hot as it sprayed on her exposed skin. Janey rolled off the bed on to the floor, where she began to crawl clumsily towards the door. Behind her, Dyer was lying face down the bed, rasping and gurgling, as his lifeblood seeped steadily onto the slick plastic sheeting. To Janey, the journey to that doorway had the treacly slowness of nightmares. She fully expected to reach the doorway, only to be confronted by the large man with the Hawaiian shirt, who had promised to skin them both.

She reached the door and used the frame to pull herself up to her unsteady feet. Things had faded to silence on the bed behind her, but she did not dare turn around, just in case she found herself face-to-face with something unspeakable. Instead, she began to make her way out of the room and onto a large dusty upper landing.

Janey found herself standing upon a floor which was covered with large mason jars. Dark splatters stained the area of the floor between each glass container. Thankfully, it was too dark to see what had been preserved in the glass containers, but the smell of pickled death on that stifling landing was overwhelming. It stank of spoiled meat and chemicals. In response to the stench, Janey felt a rising convulsion in her stomach, and she retched, splattering the floorboards with hot, bitter vomit.

Wiping her mouth, she hurried down the stairs to the ground floor.

As she stepped off the stairs, Janey found herself in a grubby kitchen area, where a small fire was smouldering in the stone hearth.

On the grey ashen corners of the fire, she could see the scorched fragments of her clothes. Beyond the fire was a single wooden door. Moving quickly and as quietly as she could, Janey approached the door and peered out of it. She discovered that it led to the dusty courtyard. This was all the opportunity she needed.

After a brief glance, to check that nobody was around, she stepped outside, and had to shield her eyes against the fierce sunlight. From this new location she could see that the house stood alone in a dry basin of land, with no other house or feature for miles. A single dirt track led away from the property, heading south like a a dry river bed leading back to the sea.

Janey knew then that her only option of escape was to follow that track and hide from any approaching vehicles.

39

At the same time as Janey Bernal was discovering her handcuffs, Leighton was cramped in the back seat of a cruiser, his hands also painfully cuffed behind him. Unfortunately, unlike Janey, he did not possess the ability to squeeze out of his restraints. The heat was stifling in the locked car, and Leighton found himself struggling to breathe.

John Ross, the senior officer who was driving the car, was confident Gretsch would probably reward him with a week's holiday for bringing this crazy old bastard in.

'Please, guys,' Leighton tried to lean forward to engage the two officers in the front of the car, 'the girl on that bus is in real danger. Can you just radio in, just ask that a car pulls the damn thing over?'

'Shut up!' shouted Harold Dean - the passenger side cop, who was playing a game on his mobile phone - without turning around.

'It's true,' Leighton continued, 'I've been investigating the bus and-'

'Investigating?' Ross laughed almost too loudly.

'She could die!' Leighton shouted - his mind suddenly filled with the endless horrors that could fall upon Vicki, knowing that he was partly responsible for this . He had few, if any options left.

'Maybe she got on the bus to escape your stalking.' Dean said, as he turned on the air-con.

'Listen, Jones,' Ross said, with a smile, 'why don't you just get yourself an inflatable girlfriend. They stick around a bit longer than the co-eds.'

'Please help,' Leighton repeated, his voice more strained this time.

'Shut up,' Dean said, and made a mock yawn. 'You're getting boring, old man. There's no need to go on and on.'

'Yeah,' said his partner, turning around. 'Maybe you should just sit back, and - Oh shit, shit! Pull over, Ross!'

Ross glanced in the rear view mirror to see Leighton's rapidly darkening face, and his head lolling on his chest. His eyes had rolled to white slits in his face, and saliva was pouring from his mouth to form a vertical puddle on his pale blue shirt.

'Fuck,' Ross shouted. 'He's having a goddam seizure or something; we can't have him die while in custody. That would be all we need.'

The cruiser came to a stop at the roadside, and both police officers climbed clumsily out of the vehicle. There was no noise from Leighton as he was dragged out of the rear seat by Ross.

Almost as soon as he was out of the vehicle, Leighton's legs gave way, crumpling beneath him, and he tumbled backwards on to the dusty roadside.

'Dammit, Dean, help me out here!' Ross called to the younger officer.

'What do you want me to do?'

'You hold him upright, and I'll get his cuffs off - and keep a look out for cars. Anyone stops, we say he's D&D. Okay?'

'Sure,' Ross said, and crouched over Leighton, pulling him to his feet. He was a dead weight, and the police officer struggled to hold him upright, while his colleague moved behind him to unlock the steel handcuffs.

Leighton performed the action so swiftly the officers barely knew what had happened. While Ross was busy unlocking the cuffs, Leighton let out the breath he had been holding, and let his half-lidded eyes fall on Ross's holster, about four inches in front of him. As soon as one hand was free, he let if fall forward, and pulled the Beretta from the holster.

Throwing his head backwards, Leighton smashed it into Dean's nose. At the same time, he saw sudden horror spread across Ross's face, and shot him in the foot. He then spun around and threw the dust he had gathered when he had been on the ground, into Dean's face. Seizing the moment, Leighton stepped behind him and slammed his foot into the back of Dean's knees, forcing him to fall forward on to the ground.

He then pushed the barrel of the pistol to the back of his head.

'Okay, young buck, I want your gun and your car keys, and I want them now!'

40

The stocky man, who had pulled a kicking Vicki onto the bus, threw her into the first seat behind the driver, and sat alongside her, blocking her in with his body. The dull reek of sweat emanating from his body was almost overwhelming.

Moments earlier, the bus had jolted to a stop, and Vicki had tried to wave it on again. Twisting one arm up her back and gripping her throat with the other, he had hauled her on to the bus, and thrown her into the first available seat.

'What was that shit about back there?'

Vicki said nothing.

'I asked you a fucking question!' he persisted.

The man suddenly grabbed her head, tearing out some strands of hair, and twisting her face towards him.

'I just changed my mind about the bus ride,' Vicki said quickly. 'I had just realised I'd left my purse at home.'

'Sorry, our tickets are non-refundable, honey, everyone completes their journey.'

He chuckled as he released her head, and began stroking her leg. Vicki moved instinctively away from him, and towards the window. In response to this rejection, the large man sighed impatiently, and slapped her hard on her face.

'Now, you play nice, or you'll get another tap, okay?'

It was in that moment Vicki almost fainted. She had caught glimpse of a thick, gold chain, hanging like a glamorous noose around the neck of the man. Along the chain, several rings of various sizes and shapes had been threaded. The third one from the end was a small gold band studded with garnets - it was the ring she had bought Laurie for her twenty-first birthday.

'Did you fucking hear me?'

Vicki nodded, her skin red and stinging.

'Good, now, take off your jeans!'

'Okay,' Vicki said. 'Just don't hit me again.'

As she undid the top button of her jeans, the large man began moaning and rubbing his crotch.

'I'll hit you often as I want, honey.'

Vicki shuddered as she leaned forward to untie her shoes. Undoing one shoelace, she then slipped her mother's compact pistol from her sock, and undid the safety catch. Sitting upright, she pointed it at the large man. His expression darkened, and he made a raging lunge for her.

Vicki fired the gun directly into his stomach, sending a mist of blood on the face of the elderly man in the seat opposite. The force of the shot knocked her attacker off the seat and on to the aisle, where he sat like a sullen child. The bus, which had swerved momentarily causing angry horns to blare, resumed its course.

'Somebody kill this bitch!' he screamed, as blood oozed through his fingers.

A clear polythene bag was immediately thrust over Vicki's head from the seat behind, and some type of cable looped around her neck. Within seconds, it was pulled tight, choking her, while she sucked desperately at the plastic shroud. She was already beginning to see black spots form in her field of vision, when she realised what she needed to do.

Twisting her body to the side, Vicki pointed the gun at the back of her seat and fired three shots in succession. The powder from the blast scorched the skin of her back, etching it into her skin like a sweeping tattoo.

The cable around her neck tightened for a second, then grew loose. Vicki pulled it from her grazed throat and gasped for air, as she ripped the mask off. Glancing to the aisle, she saw the large man on the floor was holding his bleeding stomach with one hand, while struggling to open a butterfly knife with the other.

Beyond him, the elderly man was trembling, as he fiddled with a rubber mouthpiece and large metal gas bottle.

Turning desperately around, she saw two dead men in the seat directly behind her. One had taken a shot to the face and a smear of blood, brain, and bone rose up on his headrest, like a grotesque thought bubble; the other had fallen to the side, and was now blocking the aisle. Beyond him were several grunting passengers, clambering over the corpse in a desperate attempt to reach her.

Vicki knew she had seven bullets left in the clip – not enough for all the attackers. Time seemed to stop almost entirely. For a moment, she considered turning the weapon on herself, but then she remembered what Leighton had told her: *they will stop, if they are caught, if they burn themselves out, or if they are killed.* Somewhere in the back of her mind, she heard her friend Laurie Taylor's laughter, rich and sweet. These inhumane creatures could not be allowed to continue, or disappear back into the concealing folds of society.

From somewhere out in the real world, she heard the distant swelling wail of a police siren.

'Fucking kill her!' the large man screamed again in rage and pain. In the moment it had taken Vicki to consider her limited options, he had opened the knife and thrown it at her. It flew through the air and the blade sunk deep into Vicki's right bicep. A bright flash of pain tore through her entire arm and she almost dropped the gun. Instead, with the knife still fixed in her flesh, she used her trembling left hand to cup the weapon, and took careful aim at him.

'This is for my friend, Laurie!' she said solemnly, and fired the weapon at the centre of the large man's chest.

This time, the gunshot silenced him. Vicki stood up and turned, not to the rear of the bus, but to the front. Knowing she only one chance she held her arms steady and fired. Both shots hit the driver in the back. As he slumped over the steering wheel, the bus skidded and lurched sideways. The momentum of the fully loaded vehicle hitting the curb at the strange angle sent it rolling sideways, flipping over in the process. As the vehicle crashed against the landscape, five of the passengers were instantly thrown out of the smashed windows, two were crushed by over three-thousand pounds of the metal death-trap they had created; the bus continued to roll before it stopped, nose down in a dried out creek, the only sound coming from the one wheel which was still spinning.

41

Leighton had raced back along Route 10, praying his intuition had been right, and the bus hadn't left the road yet. He had checked the cop's revolver to discover it only contained two rounds. His radio was crackling with intermittent bursts of activity, most of concerned with apprehending him. Leaning forward, he picked up the radio handset, and took a deep breath before he spoke.

'Control, this is Leighton Jones - former detective with Oceanside. I have commandeered this vehicle in the pursuit of a major group of felons.'

For a moment, there was radio silence, then an angry crackle. A nervous voice spoke to him.

'Mr. Jones, you are not in a position to commandeer anything. Please pull the vehicle over immediately.'

'I am travelling east along Route 10 in pursuit of a silver bus, licence plate number 6BTK021.'

'Mr. Jones, we need to speak to you regarding a serious assault on two police officers. Please pull the vehicle over, and await the arrival of the police.'

Leighton's eyes remained fixed on the road ahead. 'I cannot do that. Please send assistance.' He returned the radio to the dashboard, and dragged a hand over his face.

When he reached the Desert Centre junction, Leighton found the traffic was much denser. Up ahead spotted the dull metal of the bus. Panicking that he might lose them, he switched on the sirens, and began to weave through the staggered vehicles. All around him, horns blasted and lights flashed, but Leighton Jones was oblivious. His mind remained locked on the fact he seemed to be destined to fail to protect everyone he cared about.

He caught up with the bus, just as it left the highway, and took a steep exit ramp for the Corn Springs Road. This was a road which Leighton knew from his many Sunday drives - nothing more than a deserted dusty track running deep into the mountains, ending in Corn Springs Farm.

As the cruiser drifted along the exit ramp leaving the highway, Leighton could see the bus only a few hundred yards ahead. His frantic hand reached out and grasped the radio again.

'Control, this is, Jones. I've left Route 10, and am now heading due south on Corn Springs Road. I have a visual on the vehicle.'

Leighton pressed his foot down, and the car lurched towards the swerving bus, which sent up a cloud of dust in its wake, as it roared ahead of the police car.

Leighton's eyes widened in horror, as the bus suddenly lurched across the road, and shuddered on the stony verge, before swerving back across the road. It seemed to hover for a moment on the edge, before slipping off the road entirely, and vanishing.

The cruiser skidded to a stop at the point where the bus had left the road. Leighton left the engine running, and the lights on.

He stumbled out of the car and made his way to the roadside, where he saw the bus lying sideways a few hundred yards down the creek. Without hesitation, he scrambled down the steep slope towards the upturned vehicle. He was more than halfway there when he realised the gun was still in the car, but it was too late to go back.

Struggling to stay on his feet, Leighton navigated the rough, dusty terrain. He stumbled and slipped, tearing his hands on thorns and rocks. The bus had left a giant scar on the landscape as it slid nose-first into the valley, and Leighton used this channel as a path. The route was strewn with debris and several bodies. As he approached, he saw the doors of the luggage compartment had been ripped off in the crash, leaving a long rectangular cavity in the belly of the vehicle. Further corpses, wrapped in plastic sheeting and duct tape, had gathered at one end of the cavity.

It was then the acrid smell of burning rubber and diesel found Leighton like an insistent ghost, dragging him back to his past. He stood hypnotised by the smoking vehicle, as if it were some modern wicker-man. He wanted to rush to the nearest door and clamber inside, but history seemed to have doubled back on itself again. Once more he found himself faced with a burning vehicle, and the prospect of losing someone else he loved. His feet might as well have been nailed to the ground.

42

It was the strong chemical smell which drew Vicki out of the fog of unconsciousness. She opened her eyes to find she was pinned beneath the hulking dead body of the large man she had shot minutes earlier. The bus was lying partially on its side with Vicki pressed against the window beneath her. Her lower body was crushed beneath the weight of the body, which was leaking blood and fluids on to her jeans.

Twisting her head to one side, she felt a searing pain rip down the left side of her upper body. She tried to shift the man away from her, but was unable to move her right arm.

A glance to the side revealed the steel-handled blade was still embedded in her arm only deeper than before. Using her left arm she tried gripping the headrest to pull her lower body free. It was useless; his weight too much for her one limb to carry. She sobbed in pain and rage, then gripped the seat and tried again. Her legs shifted a little, and Vicki whimpered.

That was when she realised that someone was staring at her. The elderly man who had been sitting in the opposite seat was now standing over her. There was a strange expression on his face - a mixture of fascination and contempt.

'Please ... I can't move,' she said.

'I doubt your struggle will do much good. You hideous little cunt!' He then spat on her. 'I'd cut your throat right now, like I've done to silence my injured colleagues, but not you - I'd much prefer you suffered and screamed. It's such a beautiful and pure sound. Language is a mongrel tongue, corrupted by every civilisation, but our screams remain pure and honest.'

As he spoke, the elderly man began to pour fluid from a brown medicine bottle all over the surrounding seats. Vicki closed her eyes, and heard the scratch of a wooden match as the scent of sulphur filled the air. She opened her stinging eyes to see the nearby seats covered in bright, dancing flames.

As the man struggled down through the mangled bus, he laughed, and called back to her. 'When the fat man lying across your legs begins to burn, his body will melt into yours and you'll be fused with him forever. I think Wendell would have liked that idea. They say burning is the worst way to die you know,' he said gleefully. 'I'd love to stay and watch, but I have important work to do.'

Vicki closed her eyes, and let the steady crackling sounds of the fire taking hold fill her head. A hot drip of molten plastic hissed angrily by her ear, close enough to scorch her shoulder. Without opening her eyes, she silently brushed the melted disc off her blistered skin.

A strange veil descended over her mind as she accepted her fate. She had embarked on the mission for Laurie, to find her killer, and punish them. In that respect, her work was done. It was okay the journey was now over.

As she slipped further out of consciousness, and into some black void, Vicki hoped to encounter Laurie. More than that, she hoped to reach out in the gloom, and possibly find her father. In her mind, the sound of the flames taking hold became the comforting sound of the ocean; her surroundings blurred into the scorching sand, in which Vicki felt herself buried in the hot sand ... sinking deeper and deeper. All pain and thought began to ebb away.

'Vicki, I'm here for you. It's okay,' the voice said softly.

I know, Vicki thought, *you're in the darkness here with me.* The darkness was swallowing her, but it felt okay.

'Listen, you need to help me,' the distant voice said, 'I need you to open your eyes.'

Vicki wanted to stay in the warm, safe abyss, but her eyes opened to find Leighton looking at her, his face soot covered, skin bleeding, and eyes concerned. She realised he had somehow, extinguished the fire and dragged the heavy man off her legs.

'Hey there,' he patiently urged. 'I need you to reach up to me. Can you do that?'

'We were right,' she said groggily.

'I know.' Leighton nodded. 'But, you need help Vicki, so you must reach for me, okay? Do you think you can do that?'

Vicki slowly raised her left arm towards the retired detective, who gripped her wrist, and drew her safely towards him.

Once she was out of the confinement of the seat, Vicki could see for herself the carnage surrounding her. More than a dozen bodies were as she had been – crushed or pinned against the windows on the driver's side. A couple of them who had been wearing seatbelts remained strapped into their seats. Almost all of them had their throats cut.

'Come on,' Leighton said, as he slipped a supportive arm around her waist. 'this way.'

He led Vicki towards the burst skylight on the ceiling he had clambered through, but as she was struck by a sudden thought she suddenly stopped. Vicki then turned around and reached back to where the large man lay. She reached over to him and then yanked the cluster of collected rings off his neck.

By the time Leighton had half-dragged and half-carried Vicki back up to the dusty road, she was struggling to remain conscious. Her shirt was nothing more than a red glossy rag, which seemed to be wicking away her blood. Leighton had hoped to drive Vicki directly to the nearest hospital then hand himself in, but when they reached the road, he discovered the police car was gone.

'Shit!' Leighton kicked at the ground.

'The last one escaped,' Vicki slurred, without fully opening her eyes. 'He started the fire on the bus.'

'It's okay,' Leighton said. 'The road is a dead end, and the police will be here soon.'

Wincing against his own pain, Leighton helped Vicki to sit on the dusty roadside. He then sat beside her, with one supportive arm around her shoulder. Vicki tapped weakly at his leg, and he looked at her. She still had her eyes closed, but she began to speak.

'You came through, Leighton - you saved me.'

'No, miss,' he said softly. 'I think it's the other way around. But, just you rest.'

It was at that moment the orange jeep swerved towards them. It screeched to stop, and a wild haired man stumbled out of it.

'Are you Jones- the one who was speaking on the radio?' he called across to Leighton, who nodded cautiously.

'Where's the bus?'

'What?'

'They took my wife! Where's the damned bus? I've been scanning the police channels. You said it was here!'

'The bus is down there.' Leighton nodded to the ravine. 'But, there's no woman on it.'

Mike Bernal grasped his skull, pacing backwards and forwards in desperation.

'Listen,' Leighton said calmly. 'Somebody from the bus got away. They took the police car I was using. Maybe they took her.'

'Fuck!' Mike screamed and punched the dusty orange jeep.

'Hey,' Leighton called to him, 'this road doesn't go anywhere, other than to a couple of farm buildings. They can only be a few minutes ahead of us.'

'Okay.' Mike nodded with renewed hope, and started back towards the jeep.

'She'll have a better chance of surviving, if we come with you,' Leighton said, as he helped Vicki to her feet. 'I think I can help.'

43

Janey had only just started on her journey along the dusty track, when she saw the approaching police car, and felt the sudden deluge of hot tears drench her face. She turned around and ran back towards the house, waving wildly with one arm while covering her breasts with the other. The car pulled up in front of the farmhouse and screeched to a stop.

As the dust settled around the hot vehicle, a small, elderly looking detective got out of the car and glanced all around, before walking sternly towards the woman. The strange expression on his face, suggested he was both surprised and bemused by Janey's appearance.

'Thank god you're here,' she blurted, tears of relief already washing over her grazed face, 'my name is Janey Bernal, and I was abducted. There was this bus, like a Greyhound, I was drugged and taken here, and-'

'Did you call the cops?' the man asked flatly. 'It sounds like they're on their way.' He cocked his head listening to the rising wail of distant sirens.

'No, it wasn't me,' Janey said, 'there was no phone. I was in there just-'

'Is there anyone else here?' he interrupted.

'No, just me, but I think that others were killed here because-'

The small man held up a hand to silence her. 'I have one question for you, ma'am?'

'What?' Janey frowned.

'What the fuck did you do to Mr Dyer?'

Janey took a moment to realise the man standing before her was one of the men from the bus. She felt her bladder weaken.

The man's eyes were locked on her, cold and still, as he pulled the long knife from the waistband of his trousers.

'You should accept you will die here today - it is your destiny. But, first, you will serve as a crude bargaining chip.'

44

As Leighton drove the orange jeep cautiously into the yard at the front of a farmhouse, he saw the police car abandoned to one side of the building. Despite his expectations, he found that Mike Bernal's wife was alive and standing on the porch of the house. Behind her, however, was an elderly man holding what looked like a blade against the shining skin of her neck.

Leighton, his face ashen, stopped the car, and stepped carefully out of the jeep. Vicki remained slumped, semi-conscious, in the passenger seat.

'Well, it looks like the nasty little bitch got herself a sugar daddy,' the elderly man called.

'What do you want?' Leighton asked, his voice strained and weary. 'Whatever it is, we can make a deal, and you can let the woman go.'

'Oh, you poor fool.' The man laughed. 'I'll leave here, with both women and that jeep.'

'There's a perfectly good police car right there.' Leighton nodded to the cruiser. 'It'd be faster.'

'And easily tracked from the air, too. No, an inconspicuous old jeep will suffice. Now, open the driver door, then step back in front of the vehicle!'

Leighton, without any other options, did as he was told, returning to stand dead centre in front of the car.

'Now, place your hands on your head and kneel down. If I see you move, I will give this bitch a cheap fucking nose job.'

Locking his fingers on his head, Leighton knelt in the dust.

The elderly man pushed Janey out in front of him like a shield, and they moved around Leighton and towards the jeep.

As Janey neared the vehicle, Leighton mouthed a silent prayer she wouldn't recognise it. If she did, no vestige of it showed in her face. He knew he had to keep the attention on himself.

'They'll find you,' Leighton called. 'Then, it all be over. We know how the bus operated.'

'You deluded imbecile.' The man smiled, and turned from the car to Leighton. 'You think this was just about some fucking bus?' He then looked wistfully to the distance and grinned. 'Social networks are a marvellous technological development, don't you think? They allow all sorts of markets to flourish ... and grow. Our ten-thousand subscribers aren't limited to a fucking bus.'

Keeping the blade held before him, the man pushed Janey into the front of the open jeep. He then clambered in after her, pushing her against Vicki's unmoving body. Turning the key, the small man started the engine, rolled down the window and leaned out of it.

'Now, before I go,' he called to Leighton, 'I want you to see something very special. You ever see one bullet pass through two skulls?'

'Please ...' Leighton began, but he didn't need to complete the sentence, because he saw Mike Bernal rise up like a spectre from the back of the truck and fire his pistol through the rear windshield into the back of the man's head. A red spider web appeared in the windscreen, and Janey let out a long scream.

In the chaotic moments that followed, six police cars raced into the farmyard shrouded in a cloud of dust, while overhead, a police helicopter droned in demented circles. The arriving SWAT team shouted various instructions, as they formed a wide circle around Leighton, who remained kneeling in the dust. Within a few seconds, a range of carbines and assault rifles were fixed on him. Janey and Vicki were helped out of the jeep to awaiting cars, while Mike Bernal was forced to lie face-down in the dirt behind the jeep.

From somewhere in the distance, the banshee wail of approaching ambulances began swelling to a crescendo. Gretsch, who was wearing full tactical dress, jumped clumsily out of a police vehicle, and crouched by the side of a cruiser, then glanced nervously at Leighton.

'Hey, Chief,' Leighton called breathlessly across the yard to his former boss. 'Looks like there was a bus full of killers after all.'

Later on, it would be denied both privately and publicly by the Oceanside P.D., but eventually, a formal competency inquiry would conclude that it *was* Captain Gretsch who saw Leighton rub his bleeding shoulder, and intentionally shouted, 'He's going for a gun!'

This *mistake* ended not only Leighton's life but Gretsch's career.

The three loud shots hit Leighton Jones in the chest, and he fell backwards in a fine mist of blood.

As he lay gasping for breath in the hot dust, Leighton saw what he would consider two of the most important things in the whole world. The first was Vicki, being lifted by stretcher to safety, with a clear hemisphere of an oxygen mask fastened to her face. She was alive, and she was safe. That was good enough. Peering at her, Leighton felt his life slipping away like the fading remnants of a dream, and his fingers twitched upon the dry ground. He smiled a little, and let his head roll back to face the heavens, where the final image his closing eyes saw was the small, swooping circles of an expectant Merlin hawk, dancing expectantly in the sky above him.

45

The Eternal Hills Memorial Park looked pretty in the morning sunshine. It was located seven miles to the north of Oceanside, with a view of the distant waves.

As she laid the flowers on the ground so she could lock the door of her parked car, Vicki noticed the air felt similar to the day she and Leighton had first travelled together, up to Barstow. This thought came with a surge of emotion which threatened to knock her to the ground.

Steadying herself, she took a deep breath, and leaned against the warm metal of the car for a moment. The doctor had placed her bandaged arm in a neoprene sling, and told her not drive for several weeks, but she had ignored him. She had simply pulled the throbbing arm out of the sling while driving, leaving the impotent support around her neck like a burst bicycle tyre. The other options were taking a cab, which she couldn't afford, or taking an intercity bus - something she would never do again.

Turning around, she surveyed the serene beauty of the cemetery - lush, green grass beneath a perfect sky. Somewhere in the distance, a sprinkler whispered to life. Vicki glanced at the paper map of the cemetery for a moment, then picked up the bouquet of flowers, and made her way slowly to the graveside.

Following the map, she found herself standing at a shaded spot beneath an apple blossom tree. It was only September, but some of the curled blossoms had already began to float gently down to rest upon the neatly cut grass.

The simple, polished headstone before her was white - clean and honest like the man whose name it bore.

Vicki knelt down before the grave, thinking the company had done a good job of matching the two engravings, despite being separated by so many years.

She didn't look around to see if anyone might overhear her.

'Your dad didn't believe he was a good man,' she said softly, 'but we know better than that, don't we?' As she spoke, Vicki wiped the hot tears dripping from her nose. 'He told me once he always wanted to bring these for you.'

Placing the oversized daises next to the headstone, Vicki winced, as she adjusted the sling on her right arm. A small golden ring, encrusted with garnets sparkled on her finger as she gripped the bandage.

'You were good enough for me, Leighton Jones,' Vicki said through the tears. 'You hear me, god dammit? You helped me more than you know - I've got out of my mother's house, you know - I'm renting my own little place.' She wiped at her wet cheeks. 'I've got my own little patch, and I'm keeping it free from the mess of the world, like you said. You saved us all, Leighton … you saved us all.'

Epilogue

It was a hot afternoon in West London. As he leaned out of the small balcony to smoke a pre-dinner joint, Joshua Miller could smell roasting garlic from an open kitchen window. He was dressed in a pair of rolled-up linen trousers and sandals. From another balcony, he could hear the mellow sound of Bob Marley singing "Stir it Up," while from somewhere across the city, the sound of a siren rose, like the moan of a captured phantom. Joshua smiled and took a long drag on the cigarette. Much as he loved the vibe of the city, he and Claire would soon be leaving it behind for an entire month.

His flat was on the inner side of a circular building of English red brick. Built in the 1930's, for families hoping to escape the depressing familiarity of traditional homes, it was now the preserve of the city's bright and fashionable young things. Far below in the grassy courtyard, a group of tanned young ladies in floral dresses were lounging on blankets, sharing cocktails, and browsing designer shoes on a selection of digital tablets. As his eyes wandered over them, Josh mentally ranked them based on attractiveness. Then, as if sensing his indiscretion, his girlfriend called him from inside the flat.

'Josh, you've got to come through here, and see this, babe!'

Claire glanced up as her partner came into the living room, and flopped on to the white leather sofa beside her. Taking the joint from his hand, she took a puff then handed it back.

'I was just about to confirm the Portland accommodation, when this popped up.'

As she spoke, Claire tilted the iPad so he could see the display. The screen revealed a photograph of a colonial style building surrounded by tall Eastern White pine trees. The text beneath it read:

Prince of Maine Hotel - Your confirmed rate for Luxury Suite $29 per night (includes complimentary full buffet breakfast and all taxes)

'What is this?' Josh asked in a hoarse voice, as he passed the smouldering joint to her again.

'It just appeared, honey,' she said, with a shrug. 'I went to the site for the Old Colonial, like we agreed, and typed in our dates, and a new window just appeared.'

'Is it legit?' Josh tried to sound casual, but he was clearly just as intrigued as his girlfriend.

'I think so, and look at this price; we could save four hundred dollars over the ten days in Maine.'

'And it's free on our dates?'

'Yep.' Claire grinned.

'Okay then, what are waiting for?' Josh shrugged. 'Let's book it!'

Claire kissed him on the cheek, and excitedly began to type in their details.

...

Acknowledgments

Heartfelt thanks to Betsy and the team at Bloodhound Books for their tireless commitment and support.

Lightning Source UK Ltd.
Milton Keynes UK
UKOW05f0647290617
304314UK00001B/100/P